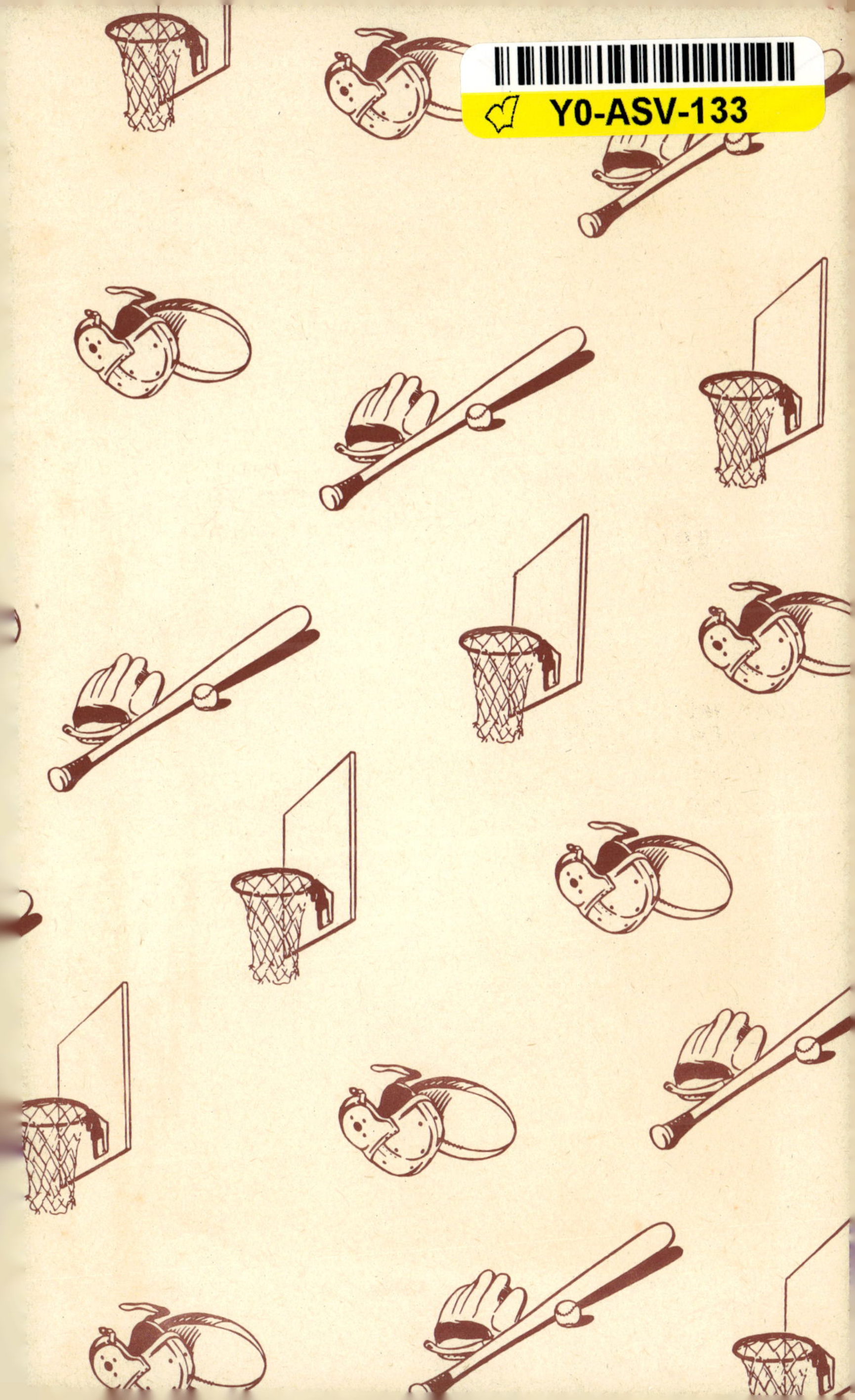

Tournament Crisis

BOOKS BY

CLAIR BEE

TECHNICAL

Basketball
Winning Basketball Plays
The Basketball Coach's Handbook
The Clair Bee Basketball Quiz Book
Basketball for Future All-American Stars
Basketball for Everyone
Make the Team in Basketball

The CLAIR BEE *Basketball Library*

The Science of Coaching
Basketball Fundamentals and Techniques
Individual and Team Basketball Drills
Man-to-Man Defense and Attack
Zone Defense and Attack

FICTION

The CHIP HILTON *Stories*

Touchdown Pass	Fence Busters
Championship Ball	Ten Seconds to Play!
Strike Three!	Fourth Down Showdown
Clutch Hitter!	Tournament Crisis
Hoop Crazy	Hardcourt Upset
Pitchers' Duel	Pay-Off Pitch
A Pass and a Prayer	No-Hitter
Dugout Jinx	Triple-Threat Trouble
Freshman Quarterback	Backcourt Ace
Backboard Fever	Buzzer Basket

"You're an American!" Tommy said fiercely. "Can't you understand that?"

A CHIP HILTON SPORTS STORY

Tournament Crisis

BY CLAIR BEE

GROSSET & DUNLAP Publishers New York

© BY MARY M. BEE, 1957

ALL RIGHTS RESERVED

PRINTED IN THE UNITED STATES OF AMERICA

To
LEONARD MULHALL
and his son
Tommy

Contents

CHAPTER		PAGE
1	The Hoop Game Bounces Back	1
2	Basketball's Forgotten Shot	10
3	State Is in the Tournament	20
4	Coaching Is a Difficult Job	30
5	Dribbling Wizard to Start	39
6	A Bench of Talented Sophs	48
7	Big Gun for the Statesmen	57
8	Five Players All the Way	69
9	How Gentlemen Play the Game	78
10	A Lesson in Sportsmanship	89
11	Subtle As a Technical Foul	98
12	We Haven't Got the Horses	108
13	The New China Tea House	117
14	A New Field House Record	129
15	Purpose of the Invasion	139
16	A Team Without a Weakness	148
17	Have a Friend—Be a Friend	158
18	Beyond the Stars to Reality	168
19	Most Valuable Player Award	176
20	Through for the Tournament	185
21	Best in Basketball History	195
22	Pictures, Cups, and Watches	207

CHAPTER 1

THE HOOP GAME BOUNCES BACK

MARY HILTON gestured toward the crowded platform. "Heavens, what a crowd! I never realized we had so many college students in Valley Falls. You'll never get a seat, Chip."

The tall youngster with the blond crew cut smiled down at his mother and moved close to her side. "That's where you're wrong, Mother," he said fondly. "You haven't seen Soapy or Speed around, have you?"

"Why, no, come to think of it, I haven't. Where are they?"

"On the train!"

"On the train? Why, they can't be! I'm sure I saw them at the Sugar Bowl."

"You saw them, all right. But they're on the train. Bag and baggage! Petey Jackson drove them out to the East End and they got on the train there. That's why I'm not worried about a seat. It was Soapy's idea."

"Well, let's just hope every person here doesn't have a friend like Soapy."

"There's only *one* Soapy, Mother."

They waited quietly, then, arm in arm, watching the restless throng below. All too soon, in the distance, they heard the warning train whistle and started slowly down to the platform. After a few steps, Chip's mother pressed his arm and spoke quickly and earnestly.

"You look fine, Chip, and you're filling out wonderfully, but I do wish you would wait a week or two before reporting for basketball. It was an awfully long football season and you've had only a few days rest. I'm afraid you'll get sick, going to all those classes and practicing every afternoon and working in the evenings, and then staying up to goodness knows what time of night with your homework."

Chip smiled and draped his arm around her shoulders. "Don't worry, Mother," he said gently. "I'll get plenty of rest—if sitting the bench can be called rest. Why, the squad has been practicing since the first of November. That means the starting team is all set."

"Then you'll upset it," Mary Hilton said confidently.

"I'll sure try," Chip said grimly. He tightened his arm and drew his mother close as they continued down the steps.

The train thundered into the station and the boarding passengers edged forward, crowding close together in an effort to gain a good position. Chip concentrated on the windows of the cars. "There they are!" he cried out. "In the sixth car. By the open window! They got the seats all right."

Smiling tenderly, Chip pulled his mother into the shelter of his arms and kissed her. Then he ran for the train, making the steps just as it got under way.

HOOP GAME BOUNCES BACK 3

He shoved the bag aboard, grasped the handrail, and turned to wave reassuringly to his mother. Mary Hilton was waving her handkerchief and saying something but she was too far away for him to hear. Chip waved again and then someone grabbed him by the arm. It was Soapy.

"C'mon, Chipper. The gang's all here." Soapy led the way, elbowing through the crowded aisle.

Up ahead, through the standing passengers, Chip could see the rest of the Valley Falls contingent; Biggie Cohen, Red Schwartz, Fats Ohlsen, and Tug Rankin grouped in the middle of the aisle. Speed Morris was not in sight.

"Gangway!" Soapy yelled. "Gangway for a guy who's got a reserved seat."

"Take your time," Biggie called. "Speed's holding 'em!"

"Yeah," Red Schwartz added, "and sitting pretty!"

"Good thing!" Soapy blustered. "I had a tough time getting those seats! I had to use a lot of ingenu—ingenu—"

"That's right," Fats Ohlsen yelled delightedly, "and that's who's sitting in 'em. Five beautiful ingenues!"

The grinning group parted, and Soapy barged through. The sight which met his eyes halted him in his tracks and he glared unbelievingly at the bevy of beautiful girls who were crowded into the facing seats.

"Oh, no!" Soapy gasped. "Oh, no!" Then he spied Speed Morris and his jaw dropped like a runaway elevator down a shaft. Speed was sitting between two of the prettiest girls Soapy had ever seen, smiling smugly and assuring them that he was extremely comfortable. "I have plenty of room," Speed said, smiling fatuously at the gorgeous blonde on his right. "This is just ducky . . ."

"Then duck, you traitor!" Soapy yelled, grabbing Speed by the hair. Soapy kept pulling until he had Speed out in the aisle. Then he slipped quickly into the space between the two girls. He smiled ingratiatingly and introduced himself. "I'm Soapy Smith! And my *friend*," he said, indicating Chip and coolly ignoring his gaping pals, "is Chip Hilton, State's All-America quarterback. I guess you've heard of *him!*"

The chorus of "Ohs" and "Ahs" and nodding of heads was enough to satisfy Soapy and bring a wave of color to Chip's face.

"Oh, I've read about *you*," the little brunette next to the window said, smiling adoringly up at Chip. "You won the Thanksgiving Day football game!"

"I saw you on television," another said shyly.

"Yeah," Soapy added, "Chip beat A. & M. for the conference championship."

"Oh, sure," Chip scoffed, "I was the only State player on the field! I won the game all by myself!"

The girl directly opposite was studying Soapy's face intently. "I've seen *you* somewhere before, Mr. Smith," she said. Then recognition dawned. "I know," she continued quickly, "State Drug! Soda fountain!"

"Sweetest job in town," Soapy drawled. "Chip works there, too. He's in charge of the stockroom."

Straddling his suitcase, Chip shifted his feet uneasily, trying desperately to think of an excuse to escape. The opportunity came when the conductor requested that the aisle be cleared and announced that an extra car had been coupled to the rear of the train at the East End and that plenty of seats were

HOOP GAME BOUNCES BACK 5

available. Chip breathed a deep sigh of relief and smiled at the girls. "Nice meeting you," he said, picking up his suitcase. "Coming, Soapy?"

"In a sec, Chip."

Chip made his way toward the rear of the train, passing Speed and the candy butcher who were deeply engrossed in some kind of a discussion. It was a long walk but the rear car was practically empty. Chip hardly had time to lift his suitcase to the luggage rack when Soapy came rushing in, followed by the candy butcher.

"Say—er—Chip," he said breathlessly, "can you lend me a coupla bucks?"

"Sure. What for?"

"Well, it's those girls. The candy guy, this fellow here, came along and practically forced me to buy a little ol' box of candy like our ninety-nine-cent special and you know how much he took me for?"

"Two dollars."

"Five dollars! Yes, sir, *five* dollars! And those gold diggers—"

"The girls?"

"Natch! They grabbed the box and opened it before I could do anything about it. And me with only three bucks to my name."

Chip smiled. "Well, you asked for it. Anyway, here's the money."

Soapy's sigh of relief was from the heart. "Thanks, Chip. You're a real pal. As far as Speed Morris is concerned, our friendship is a thing of the past. When I asked him to lend me the money he seemed to think it was a big joke. The whole gang seemed to think it was funny. Some pals! Speed was still laughing when I left. And as soon as I got up to come back here, he moved right into my seat."

Soapy turned to the grinning candy butcher. "Here's your money and I hope the government puts you in jail for profiteering." He dropped into the seat across the aisle and glared out the window.

The candy butcher grinned broadly and covertly slipped three dollar bills into Chip's hand, motioning toward Soapy. Chip nodded understandingly. Soon afterward, Speed and the rest of the Valley Falls crowd appeared, chuckling and kidding Soapy. The redhead immediately prepared to do battle, but Chip saved Speed from immediate annihilation by returning the three dollars and Soapy ruefully admitted it was a good joke. The score was tied.

Chip grinned contentedly and settled down for a nap. Seconds later, it seemed, Soapy was shaking him awake. "C'mon, Chipper, wake up! We're home!"

Chip pushed himself up and looked out the window. "Not University?"

"Yep, it's our own Almy Mammy!"

Next day, the Monday following the Thanksgiving vacation, the big topic on the campus was football; specifically, the stunning upset engineered by State over A. & M. on Thanksgiving Day. The sensational victory had knocked the Farmers out of consideration for national honors and had earned the conference championship for the Statesmen. Televised nationally as the "Game of the Week," the student fans who had found it impossible to journey to the A. & M. campus to see the big game had watched it on their sets at home.

Chip had been a key figure in the great victory and received so much attention in his classes and on the campus all morning that he decided to forego lunch and study in the library until his lab period that afternoon.

He found his favorite table unoccupied and concentrated on his work. When the librarian placed the afternoon papers on the rack, Chip got a copy of the *Herald,* University's evening newspaper, and hid behind the big spread of the sports section. But, even there, he found no escape from football. It leaped out at him from headlines on both pages in titles, subtitles, special columns, and pictures; all proclaiming State's great Thanksgiving Day victory.

"There must be *something* about basketball in the paper," he mused, turning to the back page of the section. There he found the sports news he was seeking.

SOUTHWESTERN TO DEFEND TITLE

To Play Again in Holiday Invitational Tournament

Nov. 29.—Officials at Southwestern University announced today that the N.C.A.A. champions would defend their Holiday Invitational Tournament laurels in Clinton, December 27 through December 31. Southwestern opens its season Wednesday, December 1, against Carlton and will carry a record of thirty-seven consecutive victories into the game.

Chip shook his head admiringly. "Some record," he breathed.

In the last column on the page he found a special story by Bill Bell, the *Herald's* veteran sports editor.

THE HOOP GAME BOUNCES BACK

By Bill Bell

Basketball, overshadowed by State's dramatic football season, bounces back into the center of the State sports pageant this coming Wednesday when the Statesmen

8 TOURNAMENT CRISIS

meet Southern in Alumni Gymnasium at 8:30 P.M. This will be the first contest of a tough twenty-six-game schedule. State and Southern frosh teams meet in the preliminary at 7:00 P.M.

Coach Jim Corrigan has been drilling a squad of some twenty players and has been concentrating on an all-veteran group of basketball specialists who are expected to take over where State's pigskin warriors left off, and dominate the conference. The court cast includes three seniors: Kirk Markley, Biz Gowdy, and Randy Thornhill, and four juniors, Butcher King, Dom Di Santis, Reb Tucker, and Jimmy Lu Chung.

Markley, Gowdy, Thornhill, and King were regulars last season. Jimmy Lu Chung, back from a two-year hitch in the service, is expected to fill the spot vacated by Ace Grim who was graduated last June.

Lu Chung has been sensational in the preseason drills and is certain of a trial with the starting five. The returning veteran is a master dribbler and possesses supreme confidence. Coach Jim Corrigan, without qualification, tabs Lu Chung as one of the outstanding players in the country.

Local gridiron fans will be interested to know that a trio of State football heroes will tug off their cleats and shoulder pads this afternoon and slip into basketball sneakers and report to Coach Corrigan. The trio is headed by William "Chip" Hilton, sensational sophomore quarterback, who sparked the Statesmen to the conference championship and, in the process, earned All-America honors for himself.

Speed Morris, who scampered for the winning touchdown in the last second of play against A. & M. last Thursday, is a fast, aggressive hoopster and is set to make a strong bid for one of the varsity spots. Soapy Smith proved to be a sturdy, fighting hustler for Curly Ralston's rugged line this past fall, and these same talents may earn him a spot on the court squad.

Hilton played freshman basketball last season and

averaged 34 points per game. The six-foot, two-inch star hooks with either hand and can hit with the jumper and set shot as well. It is the consensus of many fans that the youngster is better in basketball than he is in football.

If a newcomer is to break into a starting position on Jim Corrigan's all-veteran team, it most certainly will be Hilton. It would not surprise this writer if Hilton took over top hoop billing honors as soon as he can substitute the feel of sneakers for cleats. Last spring, it will be recalled by hardcourt fans, Hilton won the senior title in the National Basketball Marksmanship Tournament.

There was more but Chip had read enough. "On the spot again," he murmured. "A fellow doesn't make a basketball team just because he can shoot!"

CHAPTER 2

BASKETBALL'S FORGOTTEN SHOT

MURPH KELLY sighed wearily and closed the dressing-room door. Then he sat down on the edge of the rubbing table. "Oughta be a law!" he growled. "Football season no more than ends and it's basketball. Then it's baseball and spring football and track and tennis and golf, and then it's the middle of summer and Ralston's calling out the football squad for fall practice! Huh! That's a laugh! Fall practice in the middle of the summer." Easing himself up on the table he let his thoughts wander back over the long years he had served as State's head trainer.

And that's the way Chip and Soapy and Speed found him, deeply engrossed in nostalgic memories of State's glorious sports history. Chip and his pals paused by the door and waited for Kelly to acknowledge their presence.

"Well, what do *you* want?" he asked, swinging around to face the door. "Oh, it's you! Now what? You football guys were s'posed to turn in your gear last Friday."

"We did, Murph," Chip said gently. "We're reporting for basketball."

"I know, I know," Kelly said testily. "I read that plug Bill Bell gave you today in the *Herald*. He a friend of yours?" He waved a hand to silence the reply and continued, "Don't you fellows know when you've had enough?"

"Keeps us out of mischief, Murph," Soapy replied lightly.

"Nothing keeps you out of mischief, Smith. Well, s'pose I might as well get it over with. Take those three lockers over there by the door. How come you didn't get here on time? Poor way to start out."

"We have biology lab on Mondays and Thursdays until four o'clock, Murph," Soapy explained. He paused and then continued dryly, "And this is Monday."

"I know, I know. Well, don't worry about it. I'm used to temperamental athletes. No real harm done, anyway. Corrigan and Rockwell haven't shown up yet. Now, let's see—Hilton—size eleven shoe as I remember . . ."

The three boys dressed quickly and Chip led the way to the gym. Their sneakers made no sound on the hardwood floor and they reached the side of the court unobserved. Behind them, Murph Kelly followed as quietly, and the group paused on the side line to view the proceedings.

The squad was formed in a semicircle under the far basket, intently watching a slim, lithe player who was putting on a dribbling "show." The skill of the performer was amazing. The ball bounced this way and that, behind his back and between his legs, and from one hand to the other, as if it were held by a rubber band. The performer was a stranger to Chip, but he warmed to the broad grin the dribbler wore as he tried to please his teammates.

Chip scanned the faces of the watching players and his face lighted up as he recognized four of his teammates from the previous year's freshman squad. Sky Bollinger, Bitsy Reardon, Rud Slater, and Nick Hunter were standing shoulder to shoulder and slightly behind the varsity holdovers.

A shout of appreciation and a sudden burst of applause brought Chip's attention back to the performer. The dribbler was lying on his side on the floor now, but his uncanny control of the bouncing ball was as sure and precise as it had been while he was on his feet. "He's the greatest!" Chip murmured.

"And how!" Soapy agreed. "Now I've seen everything!"

"That's Jimmy Lu Chung," Kelly said. "Puts on a show every afternoon. The boys like it."

"Who wouldn't?" Speed whispered. "He's terrific!"

Just then, one of the players sprang forward and tried to grab the ball. But he didn't have a chance. The dribbler twisted his body with the speed and grace of a trained tumbler, and the ball suddenly appeared on the other side of his body and under the control of his other hand.

"Now you see it and now you don't!" Soapy said admiringly.

The first player who had tried to intercept the ball was now joined by other members of the squad and soon the entire group was chasing the agile entertainer. It was good fun and the light-brown eyes of the dribbler sparkled with keen enjoyment.

"I read about him in the paper," Speed said, "but I thought it was a lot of nonsense. Where was *he* last year, Murph?"

FORGOTTEN SHOT 13

"In the service. Played varsity as a sophomore three years ago. He was just fair then, but he's picked up a lot of basketball since."

"Certainly knows how to dribble," Chip said. "He's another Marcus Haynes. Haynes is old, now, but he's still good."

"And how!" Soapy said. "Has his own team and travels all over the world just as he did when he was with the Globetrotters."

"What branch of the service was Lu Chung in, Murph?" Speed asked.

"In the army. Some sort of a nuclear project. He's smart! Too smart, sometimes . . ."

The blast of a whistle brought their attention to the other basket where Jim Corrigan, State's varsity basketball coach, and Henry Rockwell, his assistant, were watching the exhibition. "All right, men!" Corrigan called. "Hit the bleachers!"

Murph Kelly led the way and Chip and his two buddies seated themselves beside him in the third row of bleachers. Sky Bollinger and Bitsy Reardon moved up beside them, grinning warmly.

"Boy am I glad to see you!" Sky whispered. He nodded toward the veterans seated in the first row. "Those guys invented the game!"

"Sure love that ball," Bitsy observed softly. "Won't trust it with a stranger."

"And they sure think we're strangers," Sky added.

"Your troubles are at an end, my friends," Soapy hissed. "We'll kill 'em!"

When the shuffling ceased, Coach Corrigan looped the whistle around his neck and cleared his throat. "Before we go to work, men, I want to introduce Chip Hilton, Soapy Smith, and Speed Morris. I guess most of you know them by reputation, if not personally. At any rate, s'pose you shake hands with them and introduce yourselves."

Chip and Soapy and Speed stood up awkwardly and shook hands with each member of the squad. Chip was known to most of the fellows, and their handclasps were firm and friendly. But when he reached the dribbler, Jimmy Lu Chung merely nodded and deliberately avoided the extended hand. Chip was puzzled and a bit nettled by the incident, but he put it out of his mind when Coach Corrigan blasted the whistle.

"All right, now, three lanes and make it good. I want to see some fast, snappy passes. Give 'em a lead and hit 'em high on the shot!"

The squad was in high spirits, driving hard for the basket, yelling for the pass, and cheering each shot. The ball flew fast and sure from player to player, the only hitch in the rhythm coming when Chip, Soapy, or Speed were directly in the action.

"Atta baby, Kirk! Nice shot!"

"C'mon, Randy, hit me, baby! Hit me!"

"Nice goin', Butcher ol' kid. Gimme that apple!"

"I've got it, Biz! C'mon in, Jimmy! Wow! What a shot!"

"Yea, Reb! Nice rebounding!"

"Give it to Dom, Butcher! Give it to 'im!"

Bitsy Reardon was right behind Chip in the passing line. "See what I mean?" he murmured. "They don't even know we've got names."

Chip saw, all right, but he wasn't worried about names right then. He had found out in the first couple of minutes that he was far from being in shape. Football was tough, but this was tougher. In football, when his team had the ball, a fellow got a rest between downs and in the huddle and coming up to the line. And when he was on the defense, he could rest until the other team did something with the ball. . . . Not so here!

In basketball, a player kept moving all the time and had to be on his toes every second! Offense *or* defense! This was man-killing stuff, unless you had worked up to it through a long training period. . . .

Corrigan was a good coach and he didn't intend to run his new recruits into the ground and risk ruining their feet in the first few days. "Hold it!" he called. "Hilton, Smith, Morris! Drop out for a few minutes Take a rest!

"O.K.! Nice going! Now, let's have a fast ten minutes on the deep figure eight. Keep driving to the basket and then fan out to the corner and up the sides. Markley, Thornhill, King, Gowdy, and Lu Chung at this end of the court.

"Rock, you take Di Santis, Tucker, Bollinger, Slater, and Reardon down at the other end. Twenty passes before a shot, now. Let's go!"

Chip and Soapy and Speed clambered thankfully into the bleachers and sat down beside the trainer. Murph was glumly watching the weave pattern the teams were executing.

"It's a veteran team, Chip," Speed said resignedly. "Looks as if the coach has his starting five all set."

"Quiet!" Chip warned. "Pay attention! Corrigan will throw us off the squad before we're on it."

The five players Coach Corrigan was drilling were almost letter-perfect in the control-ball weave. They made few mistakes and these were covered up so quickly they were hardly noticeable.

Kirk Markley and Randy Thornhill were unquestionably fine players and the three years they had teamed up in varsity play had given them a sixth sense, it seemed to Chip, where their moves were concerned. Markley was the bigger of the two and, strangely enough, the faster. Chip judged him to be about six-four in height and well-proportioned. Thornhill appeared to be a little under six feet but he was sturdily built.

"Markley's *good!*" Speed whispered.

"I like the way Butcher King handles his weight in the pivot," Soapy said. "Must weigh three hundred pounds!"

"About two-fifty," Chip breathed. "Looks taller than Sky."

"Sky's six-nine," Speed said, "but King looks twice as big."

Chip divided his attention between Biz Gowdy and Jimmy Lu Chung. If he was to make a starting position on this team, one of the two would have to be benched. . . .

"Gowdy's not so hot," Soapy muttered, as if reading Chip's thoughts. "Neither is Lu Chung."

"Can't tell until you see them scrimmage," Speed said.

Down at the other end, Bollinger, Slater, and Bitsy Reardon were having trouble. Even a novice would have noticed the difference in the passing of the two teams. Corrigan's squad handled the ball smartly and moved freely, while Rockwell's group fumbled frequently because of erratic passing. Reb Tucker and Dom Di Santis were obviously upset and out of sorts because of the play of the three sophomores.

Corrigan kept them going, counting up to twenty-five, thirty, thirty-five, and finally up to sixty passes

FORGOTTEN SHOT 17

before a shot. Then he called time and both teams trooped wearily to the bleachers.

"I'm bushed just watching," Soapy said, breathing heavily in sympathy with the tired players. "I'm beginning to think I'm an old man."

Corrigan walked over in front of the bleachers. "Now," he said, twirling the ball in his hands, "while we're taking a breather, I want to talk a little bit about shooting. All this passing we've been practicing is of no value unless the shooter can hit. Now you fellows aren't bad shooters up to twenty feet or so—but we haven't got a man on the squad who can hit from the outside.

"Holding the ball and waiting for a good shot is sound basketball and you fellows do it well. But if we don't find someone who can hit from a distance, we're going to have to face floating defenses and zones every time we step on the court.

"Now, perhaps this isn't fair, since this is Hilton's first day at practice, but he's got the best set shot I ever saw and I'm going to ask him to demonstrate it. All right, Chip?"

"Soapy has a better set shot, Coach . . ."

Corrigan smiled. "I've never seen Smith shoot, Hilton, but I *have* seen you."

"Go ahead, Hilton!" Kelly growled. "Show 'em how to shoot!"

Chip stepped carefully down through the players and took the ball. His heart was thumping like a drum, and while he waited for Corrigan to continue, he twirled and tested the ball in his long fingers.

"Don't worry about *making* the shot," Corrigan said. "I'm interested only in form. Now you backcourt men take a good look at basketball's forgotten shot. Pass the ball back after the shots, will you, Rock?"

Rockwell dropped back under the basket and waited expectantly while Chip bounced the ball on the floor three or four times. Chip got set and let the ball go from about fifteen feet—and missed the whole works, basket and all. He fired two more with the same result.

"Try it slow motion, Chip," Corrigan said kindly, "and loosen up." He turned to the bleachers. "Now let's check the shot. Chip's feet are about eight inches apart and nearly on a line. His knees are flexed and the body is inclined forward. The elbows are close to the sides and the ball is held with the fingers well spread—and even with the eyes.

"Note Chip's concentration on the basket. He's aiming the ball just as you would aim a gun, and focusing his eyes on an imaginary spot in the middle of the ring."

Chip had been self-conscious in the beginning, but as Corrigan talked, his tension vanished.

"Now then," Corrigan continued, "watch how Chip releases the ball. He takes a little hop from the floor and the hands follow through after the ball, as if he is trying to reach up and grab the rim of the basket."

This time the shot was too long, the rebound carrying the ball straight back to the spot from which Chip had released the shot. Jimmy Lu Chung convulsed and covered his mouth with his hand but the laugh was clearly audible.

Corrigan gave Lu Chung a long, hard look and turned back to Chip. "Go ahead," he said encouragingly, "hit a few. You can do it."

Chip was loose and in dead earnest now and

FORGOTTEN SHOT

form began to tell. He made the first shot, took a long stride back until he was a good twenty-five feet from the basket, and hit another. Then he began to move "around the horn," dropping the ball cleanly through the hoop. All that could be heard now was the swish of the net as the shots zipped through the cords.

"Laugh that off!" Soapy whispered sibilantly, glaring at Jimmy Lu Chung.

Shot after shot ripped through the net and then someone began to applaud. By the time Chip reached the corner, every player in the bleachers except Jimmy Lu Chung was giving him a big hand.

Corrigan was smiling proudly, and when Chip sank the last shot from the corner, he called, "Nice going, Chip. I knew you could do it."

Chip hurried back to the bleachers, self-conscious once again, but happy that he had been able to come through. As he passed Lu Chung, he could not restrain a glance at the little dribbler. Jimmy's light-brown eyes were closed to narrow slits and it was obvious that he was venomously angry.

"There's more to basketball than practice shooting, Hilton," Lu Chung sneered.

"You're right, Lu Chung," Chip agreed amiably. "I guess the same goes for dribbling."

CHAPTER 3

STATE IS IN THE TOURNAMENT

JIMMY LU CHUNG's head jerked around and he followed Chip's progress up the bleachers. There was an angry expression on his face, and his lips were trembling with fury. Then Corrigan called the two teams back to the floor for a scrimmage and Lu Chung turned away.

"Don't worry about him," Kelly said, as Chip sat down. He tapped his head significantly. "Oversized," he whispered.

"You hear him?" Soapy growled angrily, elbowing Speed. "What goes with the guy?"

"Murph has him tagged," Speed said. "He's too smart. Chip will take care of him."

Out on the court, Sky Bollinger had lined up against Butcher King, and Chip had a chance to compare the two centers. Sky was as tall, but King's bulk made the sophomore look like a bean pole. Di Santis paired up against Markley and the two appeared to be evenly matched. But Rud Slater and his six-five height towered over Randy Thornhill at five-eleven. Reb Tucker was slightly shorter than Biz Gowdy, but Jimmy Lu Chung seemed a head taller than Bitsy Reardon.

IN THE TOURNAMENT

"I hope Bitsy shows him up," Speed said.

But the reserves were no match for the experienced varsity. Markley and Thornhill and Gowdy had played together for three years and knew their screens and plays perfectly. They held the ball until they got a sure shot close to the basket.

"Terrible basketball to watch," Murph Kelly whispered. "Almost as bad as A. & M.!"

"Don't they ever use the fast break?" Chip asked.

Kelly shook his head. "Nope, never!"

Jimmy Lu Chung lost no time trying to show up Bitsy Reardon. He took advantage of every opportunity to maneuver Bitsy into Butcher King. King kept on the move, sliding from side to side across the free-throw lane, setting up picks and blocking posts for his teammates, but Jimmy did all the driving. He kept on top of the ball by reversing when he was going away from a pass, and maneuvering himself into position for a shot whenever he got a half-step advantage on Bitsy. Most of his shots were forced, but he was outjumping Bitsy and getting the shot away. And some were hitting.

"Point crazy," Speed said laconically.

"Corrigan won't let him get away with that very long," Kelly said. "He's trying him out."

Late in the scrimmage, Corrigan excused Di Santis, Tucker, and Reardon and replaced them with the three newcomers. Now, the reserve team on the floor was made up of the same personnel which had ended up as the frosh team from the previous year, with the exception of Reardon.

There was a bit of confusion about the match-ups and Chip walked over to Biz Gowdy who was about the same size. Jimmy Lu Chung trailed Chip purposefully and belligerently, and motioned Biz to take the other guard position. "I want to play against the greatest shooter in the world," he said sarcastically, winking at Gowdy. "C'mon, Hilton. Teach me how to shoot!"

"Some other time," Chip replied calmly.

Speed lined up against Gowdy, and Soapy moved over beside Markley. Then Corrigan tossed up the ball. Surprisingly, Sky Bollinger outjumped King and got the tap. Bud Slater came in high and hard, took the ball, and immediately flipped it to Chip. It seemed like old times to Chip, as he winged the ball to Soapy in the corner and set up a screen for Speed behind Gowdy.

Speed reacted like a flash and drove so hard for the basket that Lu Chung did not have time to switch. Soapy shot a fast lead pass to Speed and the flashy speedster scored.

"My, that was easy!" Soapy exulted. "Let's try it again!"

The exuberant Soapy should have kept quiet. Corrigan blasted his whistle angrily and made the reserves walk through the entire maneuver, slow motion. Then he turned on Lu Chung.

"That was your play, Jimmy. The back man always calls the switch and you should have been watching for the pick. The next time your opponent sets up a post block behind one of your teammates, and you think the cutter will get away, call the switch and call it loud! Then pick up the cutter and stick with him. Understand?"

That incident fired the varsity and they poured it on the hapless sophomores; held the ball on the offense until they cleared a man for a wide-open shot, and on the defense, used a loose man-to-man alignment which was almost a zone.

IN THE TOURNAMENT

Chip was four inches taller than Jimmy and could easily have gotten his set shot or his jumper away, but he decided to play a team game and sharpen up his passing. So he continued to feed his teammates and set up the picks and blocks.

Lu Chung was quick to realize what Chip was doing and began to play a tight defense, taunting Chip in a low, sarcastic voice. "Why don't you shoot, Hilton? Or can't you hit under pressure?"

Chip didn't like the gibes and he wanted to accept the challenge, but he controlled his temper and continued to concentrate on passing and screening. But he really burned a few seconds later when Lu Chung played dummy and caught him napping. Lu Chung floated away from Chip and turned his head. Chip relaxed and passed the ball cross-court to Speed.

As soon as Chip released the ball he realized his mistake. Lu Chung yelped gleefully, dove for the ball, and got it! He continued to chortle sarcastically as he dribbled furiously toward the varsity basket.

Chip recovered quickly and took out at full speed after the speedy dribbler. Running smoothly, he gradually closed the gap. A step inside the free-throw line, Lu Chung took off for what appeared to be a simple lay-up and an easy two points. Then Chip cut loose, turned on the gas, and timed his leap perfectly. His hand was even with the basket when the ball left Lu Chung's finger tips and the interception was easy.

Lu Chung's teammates had followed the wild drive up the court and when Chip turned he saw Speed all alone under his own basket. The rest was duck soup. Chip fired the ball the length of the court and Speed dropped it in the basket.

The blast of Corrigan's whistle was far too loud to mean anything except displeasure. "All right!" he shouted. "Time!" He followed up the court until he was even with Lu Chung. "Now just what kind of basketball are we playing out here, Lu Chung? *Your* kind or *my* kind? How many times have I told you we're not using the fast break? Tell me? How many times?"

"I'm sorry, Coach. I forgot. I—"

"That's right! You forgot *that* and the rest of your teammates, too! Just because you were burned at Hilton and wanted to make a fancy play!"

Corrigan pivoted abruptly away from the chagrined dribbler and cut loose on Biz Gowdy. "And you, Gowdy! You've been playing possession basketball for three straight years, right?"

Gowdy nodded. "Yes, Coach."

"Then why didn't *you* stop Lu Chung? And if you couldn't do that, why didn't you cover the backcourt? As a backcourt player you're responsible for defensive balance, right?"

"Right! My mistake, Coach."

Not a player moved as Corrigan glanced from one varsity player to another. He was upset and angry. After a long, heavy silence he continued. "Basketball is played with the head as well as with the arms and hands and legs and feet. Smart players make good players, and players who can't restrain their impulses make poor players. All right, that's all! Think it over and come back here tomorrow afternoon prepared to play the kind of basketball we've been practicing for the past five weeks! Good night!"

Chip and Soapy dressed hurriedly and set out for State Drug. On the way they reviewed the prac-

As soon as Chip released the ball, he realized his mistake

tice, discussing the style of play. "Back to the old grind," Soapy said wearily. "We've been gone four days but it seems like yesterday. You think we'll ever get through college, Chip?"

Chip nodded. "Before you know it, chum. Wonder how Fireball and Whitty have been making out?"

"They probably own the place by this time."

They matched strides without speaking for a time, each deep in thought. Soapy broke the silence. "Why didn't you show him up?"

"Who?" Chip asked innocently.

"You know who! You gonna let him get away with the stuff like he pulled tonight?"

"I don't think it's too important, Soapy. There's room for everybody on the squad."

Soapy shook his head. "Uh, uh! That's where you're wrong. There's only room for twelve. And twelve from eighteen leaves six. And six somebodies have gotta go."

"I know, Soapy. We've got to fight, that's all."

"You mean *I've* got to fight!"

Chip slapped Soapy on the back. "That, my friend," he said fondly, "is one of the things you do best!"

A few minutes later they were at State Drug. As soon as they passed through the door, they were spotted by Fireball Finley. "Well, look who's here!" Finley yelled. "Hey, Whitty! Look! The valiants from Valley Falls!"

Chip and Soapy were greeted from all sides by employees and customers alike. Mitzi Savrill, the petite cashier and the love of Soapy's life, shook hands and assured them that State Drug had been deserted and was practically bankrupt. "The boss

IN THE TOURNAMENT

was thinking about wiring you to take another month," she said, waving a hand toward the customers who jammed the store. "Look! The place is practically empty."

Chip and Soapy took the hint and hurried to the stockroom. State Drug was the busiest store in town and most of George Grayson's competitors attributed the rush of business to his acumen in hiring prominent State athletes.

Chip found his little helper, fifteen-year-old Eddie Redding, in the stockroom. Eddie's serious face brightened like a hot July sun breaking through the clouds. "Chip! Am I glad to see you! I'm snowed under! I never missed anyone so much in my life!"

George Grayson, owner of State Drug, opened the door quietly and stood listening. "That goes for all of us," he said. "Eddie's been doing a fine job, Chip, but all this is a little over his head."

Chip whirled around. "Mr. Grayson! I'm sorry. I'll make up for it."

Grayson smiled. "Don't worry about it. Have a nice Thanksgiving?"

"Yes, sir! I guess I was a little selfish—"

"Nonsense. How's your mother?"

"She's fine. Sends her best regards."

"Read in the paper you were out for basketball. How did you make out?"

"Fine, Mr. Grayson. Soapy and I both made out pretty good." Chip fumbled for words to express his feelings. "That is, we reported for the squad. But Soapy and I were talking and we thought perhaps it wasn't fair to you—being away from the job so much. Basketball isn't nearly as important to us as our jobs. Honest!"

Grayson smiled and shook his head. "That's where

you are wrong, Chip. Basketball *is* important. Right now the most important thing for all of us—you, Soapy, and me—is for you fellows to make that basketball team. I mean it, Chip. So you just forget all about being away from the job and make the team! O.K.?"

Chip couldn't find words to reply, so he made up for it by working the rest of the evening as if his life depended upon catching up with accumulated invoices, check lists, and the proper storage of the supplies which had arrived during his absence. Before he realized it could be possible, it was ten thirty and Soapy and Fireball and Whitty showed up to slip out of their gold-and-white fountain uniforms and head wearily for Pete's restaurant and their usual after-work snack.

Pete greeted them warmly. "Hey! Look who's here! Chip! Soapy! About time you guys showed up! Place hasn't been the same. Right, Fireball, Whitty?"

Chip had no difficulty in getting to sleep that night. When he awakened Tuesday morning, Soapy's bed was unoccupied. He got up slowly, painfully aware that his muscles were tight and stiff. Before he had finished washing, Soapy was back.

"Hey, Chip! You see the paper?"

"What are you talking about? How could I see the paper?"

"Well, take a look!"

"No, you tell me. What is it?"

"State's in the tournament!"

"What tournament?"

"You know the Holiday Invitational? The tournament they hold in Clinton during the Christmas holidays? Well"—Soapy paused dramatically and then continued with a rush—"State's been invited!

IN THE TOURNAMENT

Honest! State's been invited to participate and the invitation's been accepted! How about that?"

Chip's indifference vanished. "You're kidding!"

"No, I'm not! Honest! Starts on Monday, December twenty-seven, and goes through the thirty-first. The defending champions are Southwestern. They've won it four straight times! And they've got the same team back that won it last year."

"I guess they're pretty good."

"Pretty good? Listen! They've won thirty-seven straight and a hundred and thirty some in a row at home. And listen to this! They've won the N.C.A.A. five times in the last twelve years. And the Holiday Invitational four *straight* times!"

"What other teams in the tournament have been seeded?"

"College of the West, A. & M., and Southeastern."

Soapy turned back to the paper. "And listen to this! 'Southwestern's championship five is made up of five seniors who have put together the greatest basketball record in college history. Every writer in the country picks them to repeat in the Holiday Invitational Tournament and in the N.C.A.A. championships.'"

"Upsets happen, Soapy. Winning any tournament is a tough assignment and the Holiday Invitational will have the pick of the country lined up."

"I know, but a team like Southwestern *has* to have what it takes."

Chip nodded and changed the subject. "We've got a tough assignment, too. I didn't tell you, but last night Mr. Grayson said the most important thing we had to do right now was to make the varsity."

"You think he was kidding?"

"I know he wasn't. He was dead earnest."

CHAPTER 4

COACHING IS A DIFFICULT JOB

SOAPY SMITH was a good basketball player but he wasn't top flight. And unlike most players with average skill, Soapy knew his limitations. But he loved basketball, and when he played, he gave it every bit of his enthusiasm, spirit, aggressiveness, and ability. In fact, Soapy was usually enthusiastic about everything; kept his spirits high and met adversity or good fortune with a smile. But not this morning.

At breakfast, while Chip was reading the paper, Soapy was methodically counting on his fingers, over and over again. His brow was creased and it was clear that he was mulling something over which was extremely important.

"Now what?" Chip asked. "What's the big problem?"

"You know," Soapy said accusingly. "Basketball! Basketball and State Drug and Mr. Grayson and a college education."

"I don't get it."

"Well," Soapy explained patiently, "Mr. Grayson said the most important thing we had to do was make the basketball squad, right? So, figuring *my*

A DIFFICULT JOB

chances to do that, I'm wasting my time. I'd better pack up."

"I still don't get it."

"Listen!" Soapy rested the elbow of his left arm on the table and counted off on each finger as he named a player. "One, Kirk Markley. A veteran and good, right?"

Chip nodded. "Right."

"Two, Randy Thornhill. And *he's* a senior and good. The same goes for Biz Gowdy, Butcher King, Dom Di Santis, and Reb Tucker. That makes six veterans and it doesn't include Lu Chung. Corrigan's already tabbed him as one of the best in the country and that's seven. . . ."

Chip started to say something but Soapy checked him and continued. "Take the sophomores. You're a cinch! And so is Sky Bollinger and Rud Slater and Speed and Bitsy Reardon, and that's twelve any way you figure it. . . .

"That leaves me with good ole unlucky number thirteen and that's out, so I'm out! Even if I was good enough to beat out Farley and Kepley and Kane and Flash Gibbons." He shook his head mournfully. "It ain't good."

"Maybe the coach will carry more than twelve players."

"Not a chance. I asked Murph Kelly and he said Corrigan doesn't like big squads. Nope, I'm a dead duck. Valley Falls, here I come!"

"It's not quite that bad. Mr. Grayson didn't mean 'or else!' He was trying to tell you and me not to worry about our jobs. That's all."

Soapy pressed his lips into a thin straight line. "I can't make that squad, Chip. I know it."

"We'll see," Chip said quietly. "I think you underestimate yourself. Now forget about basketball and finish your breakfast."

Chip resumed his reading, turning the pages of the morning *News* until he came to the sports page, and there, almost as if Soapy had written the article, was confirmation of the redhead's fears.

STATE READY FOR BASKETBALL OPENER

Meets Southern Tomorrow Night at Alumni Gym

BY JIM LOCKE

State will field a veteran team tomorrow night against Southern in Alumni Gymnasium. Coach Jim Corrigan has been working three seniors and two juniors as a unit for the past several weeks and has indicated that he will start the same five which carried the load most of last year. The only newcomer is Jimmy Lu Chung and he cannot be considered as such, since he was a member of the squad three years ago. The combination which will start tomorrow night has Kirk Markley and Randy Thornhill at forwards, All-Conference Bill "Butcher" King at center, Biz Gowdy and Jimmy Lu Chung at guards.

Other veterans who will most certainly see action, according to Corrigan, are Reb Tucker and Dom Di Santis. The squad will probably be rounded out with five sophomores up from the frosh team of last year: Sky Bollinger, local high school phenomenon; Rud Slater, outstanding rebounder; Bitsy Reardon, last year's captain and second leading scorer, and two of State's brightest football stars, Chip Hilton and Speed Morris . . .

Chip glanced at Soapy, hastily folded the paper, and slipped it behind him on the chair. "Come on," he urged, "we're going to be late for class."

They found the campus buzzing. The big topic was basketball. King Football is dead! Long live King Basketball!

A DIFFICULT JOB 33

"Southwestern will walk right through that tournament."

"How about A. & M.? And College of the West? And Southeastern and Dome and Wilson Tech? They're not pushovers!"

"They're not Southwestern, either."

"What's the matter with State? We've got everybody back."

"Won't get past the first round. Just an excuse for a trip. They have to have *someone* to fill out the draw."

"Well, we'll know tomorrow night."

"Know more Wednesday week when we play Southwestern."

"Be a slaughter! No one, but *no* one, beats Southwestern on their home court. They've won a couple hundred in a row at home."

"Not quite, but they've won a lot."

Chip and Soapy and Speed reported for basketball an hour early that afternoon. Their muscles were tight and Murph Kelly gave them a ball and told them to run the stiffness out. Once in the gym, they limbered up and took ten laps around the floor, and then began practicing their shots.

A little later members of the squad began to show up, one by one, and then Jimmy Lu Chung came dribbling wildly out on the court. When he saw Chip, he dribbled over beside him. "I'm ready, Hilton," he said. "Show me how to shoot! You said yesterday you would teach me some other time. *This* is some other time."

Chip smiled amiably. "I don't think I could teach you anything about basketball, Lu Chung," he said. "You've had a lot more experience than I have."

Every player on the court was conscious of the

conversation and its implications, but each continued shooting and talking as if nothing unusual was taking place. That is, all but Soapy Smith and Speed Morris. They watched every move Lu Chung made.

"How about one-hand sets?" Lu Chung suggested, dribbling to the corner, setting, and dropping the ball cleanly through the basket. "All right?" he gibed, recovering the ball. "Or am I using the wrong form?"

"Looks pretty good to me," Chip said.

"Well, then, how about a jumper?" Lu Chung dribbled back to the center of the court and then drove for the free-throw circle at full speed. He stopped suddenly, leaped into the air with the ball held at full arm's length above his head, and released it at the top of his jump with a flick of his fingers. The ball went spinning away, true and straight and right through the hoop.

Lu Chung landed on the court and turned, grinning in fake humility. "All right?"

"Perfect," Chip said calmly, conscious of the fact that Lu Chung was going all out in his effort to bait him; but conscious also of the fact that the control of his emotions would have a greater effect upon the dribbler than a burst of angry words.

Corrigan appeared at that instant and sent them into his three-lane warm-up drill, and Chip breathed a sigh of relief.

The practice session was almost a repetition of the previous day. Corrigan used Chip and Soapy and Speed sparingly, but he had no mercy for the rest of the squad. He drilled them at full speed for an hour and a half. Then he sent everyone to the bleachers.

A DIFFICULT JOB

Chip had a presentiment and he wished fervently that he could be spared what was coming. His fears were quickly realized.

"Fellows, coaching is a difficult job. There is little gratification even in winning games because there is always the next one which may be the killer. Losing is bad. But cutting a squad is worse.

"I've spent—Rock and I have spent—many long hours trying to figure who should be kept on the squad and who should be dropped. This is, as you know, the third and final cut. The other two cuts were bad enough, but this is the worst of all, chiefly because there is such a narrow margin of superiority between many of those who will remain on the squad and those who will be asked to report to Coach Rockwell here for the JV."

Chip was staring straight ahead, trying to breathe naturally. On either side, he could hear the tense, measured breathing of Soapy and Speed and he knew they were having the same difficulty.

Corrigan's voice hardened. "The following players are to report to Coach Rockwell on Thursday afternoon in the field house gym: Hunter, Farley, Kepley, Gibbons, Kane, and Smith."

It was done! Chip released a deep breath and reached over and gripped Soapy's knee. Speed lowered his head glumly and snapped a tight fist into his open hand.

Corrigan wasn't through. He began to speak again and Chip wanted to yell out that he had said enough; to let it stand and forget the details. Then the words bit through—

"With respect to you, Smith, Rock and I both feel that you haven't had a fair chance. We hope you will understand that it was necessary for us to make the decision before our first game. I'm truly sorry you couldn't have been with us during all of the preseason practices . . ."

Corrigan took a deep breath and continued, "All right, you men are excused until Thursday."

Chip tightened his grip on Soapy's knee. "Wait for me, will you, Soapy?"

Soapy nodded and swallowed. "Sure, Chipper," he managed, rising stiffly to his feet. "I'll wait."

Chip was thinking of the story he had read that morning in the *News*. "Jim Locke knew," he whispered to himself. "Corrigan gave him that list yesterday. I wish now I had let Soapy see it."

Chip and Speed didn't get much of a workout that afternoon and both were relieved. There wouldn't have been much fun in it. Late in the practice, Chip and Speed replaced Reb Tucker and Bitsy Reardon, and Lu Chung again leeched on to Chip. But this time, Corrigan was watching every move he made and Lu Chung played it straight; he concentrated on his game and never said a word.

Chip could sense the fellow's animosity and see the dislike in the narrowed eyes and grim-set jaw. He was glad when Corrigan called it a day.

Chip and Speed showered and dressed quickly and found Soapy waiting. The three buddies walked slowly across the campus and down Main Street to State Drug. Soapy did all the talking but it was painfully obvious that his gay voice and lighthearted attitude was an affectation. Speed left them at Main and Tenth, and Chip and Soapy went to work. It was a long evening.

That night, after work, Chip, Soapy, Fireball, and Whitty headed for Pete's Place, each trying to cheer Soapy up without making it apparent. But they wer-

A DIFFICULT JOB 37

poor actors and it was Soapy himself who saved the awkward situation. He checked them outside the restaurant.

"Look," Soapy said. "Let's cut out all the nonsense. I wasn't good enough and I got cut and that's that! Now, if you fellows will forget the whole thing, I'll feel a lot better. . . .

"Anyway, I'm not quitting. I'll be on that team yet! If not this year, then next year. And if not next year, the year after. Mark my words, there will come a day when Jim Corrigan and Henry Rockwell will both thank their lucky stars that good ol' Soapy Smith was around to save the day."

That did it!

"Oh, sure!" Fireball whispered breathlessly and dramatically. "The score will be tied. There will be less than a second to play and Corrigan will stalk out on the court and yell time! And then he'll have Soapy Smith paged over the loud-speaker.

"Then *you!*" He paused dramatically and tapped Soapy on the chest. "*You* will leap from the balcony and—"

"Hold it!" Whittemore said quickly. "And the band will play 'A Star Fell from Heaven'!"

Fireball apologized profusely. "Excuse me. You're so right, Whitty. Slight omission. I'm not myself tonight . . . And then Soapy will hold up both hands for silence. And when the only sound that can be heard is the rippling of the basket cords, Soapy will turn his back to the basket—"

"I know!" Whitty interrupted. "He'll turn his back and bounce the ball through his legs and through the basket and win the game and—"

"And they'll hang his shoes in the library!"

"The zoo!"

"The library!"

"The zoo!"

Soapy made a dash for the door to Pete's restaurant. "Oh, boy!" he shouted. "I'm a hero! I'm a hero!"

Inside, Nick Hunter and several cronies were seated in one of the booths. Nick greeted Soapy like a long-lost friend, although the two had never been close. "Hiya, Soapy. How did you like the surgery this afternoon?"

Soapy shrugged. "You mean bein' cut from the squad? So what! Part of the game."

"Personally, I'm kind of glad," Hunter said. "I didn't feel too good about playing on the same team with a foreigner, anyway—"

Before Soapy could reply, Chip interrupted, stepping between his pal and Hunter. "Lu Chung isn't a foreigner," he said quietly. "He was born here, and he served three years in the service. His father and mother were naturalized in this country."

"So what? What does that make him?"

"It makes him an American citizen. Just as much an American as you or I."

CHAPTER 5

DRIBBLING WIZARD TO START

PETE THORP was proud of his restaurant. The equipment was old and unattractive, but Pete kept it scrupulously clean. Furthermore, Pete never served anything he wouldn't eat or drink himself. Pete heard part of the conversation between his pal Chip Hilton and Nick Hunter but he was too busy to pay much attention. But he wasn't too busy to overlook the steaming cup of tea which the young fellow opposite the booth at the counter had left untouched. Pete followed the youth forward to the cash register to ring up the charge.

"Anything wrong with the tea?" he asked worriedly.

The stranger smiled understandingly. "No, not at all. The tea is fine. Just couldn't stomach the conversation in the booth, that's all. What's the fellow's name who just came in? The one who was talking?"

"You mean the blond—the one with the crew cut? That's Chip Hilton. Great athlete. Friend of mine. Want to meet him?"

"No, thanks. I just wondered who he was. Thanks again and good night."

Pete glanced at the booths. Nick Hunter's group was preparing to leave and Chip and his three friends were talking quietly. He waited by the cash register until Hunter's crowd had settled their accounts and then hailed Chip.

"Hiya, Chip. See by the paper you're on the basketball team."

"Not the team, Pete. Just the squad. There's a difference."

"Don't let him kid you," Fireball said. "He's on it!"

"Might be just on the squad now," Whitty added, "but he'll be on the starting five just as soon as he gets in shape."

Pete nodded. "Tellin' me! How *you* makin' out, Soapy?"

"Well, you see, it's like this, Pete. Corrigan handles the varsity, right? And Rockwell handles the JV and does all the scouting. Right? So Corrigan says to me this afternoon— He says, 'Soapy, you go down there with the JV starting Thursday and help Rockwell out.' So, bein' the kind of a guy I am—why, I'm going, going, gone!"

Pete blinked and nodded his head. Then he nodded again. "Yeah," he said. "Yeah, I've known that for a long time. Real gone."

"All right, you guys," Fireball said, banging the table with his fist. "Do we eat or sit here and gab all night?"

"That's right," Soapy said, "we've got to get in before curfew. Another one of my new responsibilities, Pete."

Later, lying awake in the room he shared with Soapy in Jefferson Dormitory, Chip wished there was something he could do to help his best pal forget the deep hurt of that afternoon. Soapy had put up a good front but the hurt was there. Chip was still trying to think of a solution when he fell into a troubled sleep.

King Basketball was still king on the State campus the next morning and everyone was talking about the game with Southern. Chip was known to almost every student, now, and he tried to avoid the sports chatter, but he couldn't miss the *sotto voce* references.

"That's Hilton. They say he's better in basketball than he is in football."

"Now I'll tell one!"

"It's the truth. You see Monday's paper? That's what Bill Bell said."

"He better be good! Southern's tough! Going to the Sugar Bowl."

"So what? State's going to the Holiday Invitational. Same difference."

"Uh, uh. Southern won the Big Twelve Conference. Got everyone back."

"So have we. We'll take 'em tonight. Especially with Hilton in the line-up. He's the best shot in the country."

Soapy met Chip in the library right after lunch and tossed a copy of the *Herald* on the table. "You see this, Chip? The story about Lu Chung?"

"No, I didn't. What does it say?"

"Read it."

STATE UNVEILS DRIBBLING STAR TONIGHT

Hardcourt Wizard to Start

By Bill Bell

Tonight, at Alumni Gymnasium, Coach Jim Corrigan will present the player he calls "One of the greatest

42   TOURNAMENT CRISIS

dribblers in the country." Although State meets Southern in a tilt which will have no effect upon conference standing, the contest will go a long way in determining the championship stature of the Statesmen, as well as the personal ability of Jimmy Lu Chung to spark a veteran team to greatness.

Jimmy Lu Chung, returning serviceman, is not unknown to State basketball fans. Lu Chung was on the varsity basketball squad here three years ago as a sophomore and returned this year to enter the junior class and complete his education.

Lu Chung is an exceptional athlete. He was so highly regarded as a nuclear science student three years ago that the Army invited him to become a member of a special group assigned to a top-secret defense project. The project completed, Lu Chung is back in school to continue his science course.

This reporter has talked to several members of State's science department and all are enthusiastic in their praise of the youngster's science ability and in predicting a great future for the brilliant student.

Chip tapped the paper. "That's a swell article. Mind if I tear it out?"

"Of course not, but why?"

"Because it's a nice write-up."

Soapy was puzzled. "What d'ya want it for?"

"I just think it's a good story, that's all."

Soapy gave Chip a long look. "I wouldn't think you'd want any part of that show-off," he said gruffly. "After the way he's been acting."

"Did you ever stop to think how you would act if you were the only American trying to make a Chinese basketball team, say in Hong Kong?"

Soapy grinned. "Now there is a real idea! You really think I could make a Chinese basketball team?" He waited for the reaction. When it was

DRIBBLING WIZARD 43

evident that Chip found his efforts distasteful, he sobered and meekly said, "Sorry, Chip. Guess maybe I'd be a whole lot worse than Jimmy Lu Chung. O.K., pal?"

"Sure. Skip it. I'm going to work. Coming?"

"Good idea. Let's go."

Both boys took advantage of every chance to repay George Grayson for his generosity in permitting them to practice and play sports and hold their jobs. Game afternoons, because there was no practice session, gave them the opportunity to repay, in part, their kind and understanding employer.

That night, Chip was the first player to don his uniform. He gave the string of his basketball shoe a final tug and leaned back against the door of his locker, acutely aware that this was the first time for many a moon that he and Soapy had not suited up together. He and Speed exchanged glances and Chip could tell that his home-town teammate was thinking the same thing.

Sky Bollinger was on the rubbing table and Mike Murphy was taping the big fellow's ankles. Sky caught Chip's glance and winked. Chip returned the wink and pushed back hard against the locker, his long fingers gripping the hard bench. This was the part that was tough. The waiting . . .

By eight o'clock everyone was suited up and Coach Corrigan came in for his pregame talk. He waited until they quieted. "Let me have your attention, fellows. One of the State traditions is the election of a captain just before the first game. So, let's get at it. Here, Murph, hand out these seven pieces of paper. Letter men only. That means everyone except the sophomores. Now, let me have the nominations."

Butcher King raised his hand. "Kirk Markley," he said, grinning at Di Santis.

Di Santis came right back. "Randy Thornhill!"

"Any other nominations?" Corrigan asked. "No? All right, here's a couple of pencils. Pass 'em around."

The pencils moved around the circle and Kelly collected the votes. Corrigan sorted them into three piles on the training table for everyone to see. One pile had but a single piece of paper while the other two had three each.

"Tie vote," Butcher King whispered jubilantly. "Co-captains!"

Corrigan verified the count. "That's right," he said. "Kirk Markley and Randy Thornhill each have three votes. Congratulations, Kirk, Randy."

"Someone didn't vote," Markley said accusingly. "How come?"

"Yes," Thornhill added. "Put-up job!"

Butcher King nodded. "You're so right!" he quipped. "I didn't vote. We happen to like both you guys."

"Time, Coach," Kelly warned, glancing at the clock.

Corrigan banged the dressing-room table with the flat of his hand and the players quieted instantly. "We'll start with Markley and Thornhill up front, King at center, Lu Chung and Gowdy in the backcourt. You fellows know as much about Southern as I do, so it's up to you. Let's go!"

Jimmy Lu Chung was the last veteran to leave the room. He paused at the door long enough to cast a triumphant look in Chip's direction. Chip smiled and immediately forgot the incident. This was his first big college game and the cheers, crowd noise, and band music thrilled him to his toes, im-

DRIBBLING WIZARD 45

bued him with an intense desire to play; to get out on the court and run Southern into the ground.

Southern was reputed to be one of the outstanding teams in the country and proved it with the blast of the starting whistle. The visitors worked a play off the center top so easily and smoothly that it didn't look as if they were trying. It was the old "guard down" play, one of the oldest in the game; center to forward to guard cutting down the same side of the court.

Corrigan and every player on the State bench saw the play coming and yelled: "Heads up! Lu Chung! Jimmy! Watch out, switch!" But the warning shouts were too late.

The Southern center outjumped King, tapped the ball to the forward Jimmy was guarding, and a speedy guard sped down the side line and took the pass under the basket for the tally. He scored before Lu Chung fully realized what had taken place.

That first play set the pattern for the game. The Southerners were opportunists, took advantage of every State mistake, and kept their errors to a minimum. When State had the ball, they switched beautifully for one another and proved to be a defensive-minded club.

State's veterans played the slow, methodical style in which they had been grooved. The set plays lacked color and dramatic action, but the style was good enough to keep the game close. With the exception of Lu Chung, who dribbled too much and shot too often, the play of the State veterans was steady, if not too effective. Lu Chung's tricky passes often threw his receiver off balance and led to interceptions. The visitors jumped into the lead and kept it throughout the game.

Chip watched every move Lu Chung and Biz Gowdy made. Lu Chung was by far the better offensive player, but defensively, he made a lot of serious mistakes. Mistakes which cost State precious points. Corrigan took him out late in the third quarter and replaced him with Reb Tucker. Thereafter, the team played better defensive ball but lacked the scoring punch to keep pace with Southern.

The only other players to see action in the dreary game was Dom Di Santis for Biz Gowdy and Sky Bollinger for Butcher King. The final score: Southern 68, State 56.

State Drug was the gathering spot for State sports fans and many of them stopped by after the game to talk basketball. Soapy, Fireball Finley, and Philip Whittemore were known to most of the customers and usually had time to participate in the conversations. But not tonight. The three athletes were on the go every second but they didn't miss the chatter.

"Southern was too good. What a defense!"

"We need someone who can score."

"How you going to score holding the ball?"

"Got something there. Bet we didn't take fifty shots!"

"I counted thirty-six passes one time before we took a shot."

"The crowd didn't like it, that's for sure."

"Same goes for the players. Biz Gowdy's a friend of mine. . . . He hates it."

Jimmy Lu Chung and Hip Farley came in a little later and sat down opposite Fireball's station. Both were strangers to Fireball and he wouldn't have given them a second glance had he not heard the name "Chip Hilton." Fireball shot a quick glance in

DRIBBLING WIZARD 47

their direction but they were evidently unaware that he was listening.

"But Hilton *is* good. *I* know."

"Just because he can play football, it doesn't mean he can play basketball."

"Listen, Jimmy. I don't mean football. I'm talking basketball. Freshman basketball. He was great!"

Lu Chung shrugged disdainfully. "Huh! Freshman basketball! Kid stuff."

"The A.A.U. shooting championship isn't kid stuff."

"Anyone can shoot if there's no one guarding him."

"I wish you would take my advice and play ball with him. He's a nice guy."

"But he isn't a basketball player. He hasn't tried a shot and I took the ball away from him twice in a row. If that old has-been, Hank Rockwell, wasn't Corrigan's assistant, Hilton would have been cut off the squad with the rest of you guys."

"Have it your way, Jimmy, but don't say I didn't tell you."

When the two boys left the fountain and reached the cashier's desk, Fireball pointed them out to Soapy. "You know that little fellow, Soapy? The Chinese fellow?"

Soapy nodded. "Sure. That's Jimmy Lu Chung, the fellow that's been needling Chip. The other fellow is Hip Farley. Why?"

Fireball told him about the conversation and Soapy hit the ceiling. "That does it!" he said angrily. "Wait until I tell Chip what Lu Chung said about Rock. Chip won't let him get away with that!"

CHAPTER 6

A BENCH OF TALENTED SOPHS

JIM CORRIGAN was young, ambitious, and proud of his profession. He loved his job and had looked forward to a successful season. The previous night's defeat had left him depressed and the result of a sleepless night was reflected in the tired lines on his face. Sitting at his desk, reading Jim Locke's story in the *News*, a deep frown of annoyance deepened the two little lines between his eyes.

STATE LOSES OPENER TO SOUTHERN

BY JIM LOCKE

Southern spoiled State's opening game of the season last night by defeating the Statesmen, 68 to 56. Coach Jim Corrigan presented a veteran team and a style of basketball which was obsolescent when this writer was in grade school.

The only interesting feature of the game was the play of Jimmy Lu Chung who sparked Corrigan's attack (?) during the three quarters he played.

Corrigan closed the paper with an angry gesture. "I'd like to punch that—"

"'Morning, Jim. Busy?"

Corrigan looked up with some annoyance but the feeling vanished when Henry Rockwell sauntered through the door and sat down on the other side of the desk. Managing a grin, Corrigan tossed the newspaper on the desk. "No, Rock, far from busy. When did you get in?"

"This morning. Early. Came in on a sleeper. Too bad about last night. What happened?"

"We couldn't score. They got out in front and we couldn't catch up. How's Carlton?"

"About like we are, I'd say. Run a lot, play man to man, and just about match us for size. I'll have the notes ready for practice."

"Going to use the JV's to demonstrate?"

"Sure! I'd like to."

Rockwell picked up the newspaper. "I see your pal is at it again."

"He's no pal of mine," Corrigan said bitterly. "Did you read it?"

"Yes, Jim," Rockwell said sympathetically, "I did. Forget it. I've been through the same thing many times. Don't let it get you down."

During the thoughtful silence which followed, Corrigan studied the face of the veteran mentor. Rockwell had been retired two years ago from his job at Valley Falls High School, where he was coach of all sports, and had accepted a position in State's athletic department. "He doesn't look his age," Corrigan was thinking. "His hair is still black, and his face hasn't got as many wrinkles as mine. Hasn't got an ounce of fat on his body, either. The old boy must be past sixty, at least. Anyway, I'm lucky to have an experienced coach like him for an assistant."

"Rock," he said at last, "do you think he's right?

Do you think we should change our style of play?"

"A little late for that, Jim. I think he's right about the need for a scoring punch. And as he says, our defense isn't good."

"What do you think we ought to do?"

"I think we ought to make a couple of changes."

"What changes?"

"Well, I think Hilton should be worked into the line-up as quickly as possible. He can shoot and he's a fine defensive player. I know he's not in shape yet, but he'll come along fast. He ought to be working with the regulars and—"

"And—" Corrigan prompted.

"And I think Bollinger and Morris and Reardon ought to see a little more action."

"Who would you bench?"

"That's a tough one, Jim." Rockwell eased himself a little lower in his chair and concentrated on an object outside the window behind Corrigan. Then he cocked an eye at the younger man and grinned ruefully. "You might not like this, but if it were me, I would bench Lu Chung. He's too erratic for the deliberate attack we're using. If we were using the fast break, yes. Slow advance and possession attack, no."

Corrigan nodded thoughtfully. "I guess you're right. He was pretty bad last night but I figured he was pressing, trying too hard."

"He'll never be a steady player, Jim. He has to have the ball."

"Trouble with most players," Corrigan agreed. "Don't know what to do *without* the ball. That's one of the reasons I use a set attack."

"You want me to scout Southwestern tomorrow night?"

TALENTED SOPHS 51

"I sure do. Tomorrow *and* Saturday. I know they'll be tough on their own court, but I want to be ready for the tournament. Just in case we do draw them. We probably will. See they won number thirty-eight last night."

Rockwell nodded his head, smiling ruefully. "And ran up a big score doing it. Jeff Habley's a peculiar fellow. Seems to get a kick out of pouring it on a team when he's got it down."

"Not very many coaches like him, that's for sure. He has the teams, though."

"He gets the players, Jim, that's all. Gets 'em from all over. Attack seems to be built around the big center, Bordon, and his captain, Rip Ralk. Both made All-America last year."

"Average around thirty points apiece, don't they?"

Rockwell pulled a piece of paper out of his pocket. "That's right," he said, reading off the statistics. "Bordon averages thirty a game and Ralk twenty-eight. Then it's Perkins with twelve, Lloyd with ten, and Munn with eight. That's an eighty-eight-point average per game for the starting five and Habley keeps 'em in the game right down to the wire."

"How big *are* they? I know Bordon's pushing seven feet . . ."

"They're big enough," Rockwell said grimly. "Listen! Bordon, six-eleven; Perkins, six-six; Ralk, six-four; Munn, six-three; Lloyd, six-two. That's an average of six-five, and knowing Habley's reputation, you can bet your life it's an understatement."

Corrigan threw up his hands. "Stop! You're scaring me to death. Let's change the subject. Do you think we can take Carlton?"

"I think so. Anyway, I'll have all the dope ready by four o'clock. See you then."

Corrigan wasn't the only one upset by the newspapers that day. Soapy found Chip, as usual, at the library and placed a copy of the *Herald,* opened to the sports page, on the table.

"You made the paper, my friend," the redhead said lightly. "Bill Bell again!"

"Now what?"

"Says one Chip Hilton would give State a scoring threat and someone to build the attack around. How do you like those tomatoes?"

"I don't!"

"Guess Bill Bell don't care whether you like it or not. You know what else? He says Bollinger and Reardon can shoot almost as well as you can. Then he gets real tough and says that it doesn't make much sense to field an all-veteran team which isn't going anywhere and keep a bench of talented sophomores on the side lines. Hot stuff, eh?"

"Sounds more like Jim Locke than Bill Bell."

"Maybe so, but that's what he said. Come on, we have biology. Three hours of dead fish and uncooked frog legs."

Jimmy Lu Chung read the papers that day, too. Every athlete likes to see his name in a line-up in the paper and Jimmy was no exception. He read the account of the game in both the *News* and the *Herald,* and then he read Jim Locke and Bill Bell. When he finished Bell's column, his face was flushed with anger. "What's the matter with Bell?" he muttered. "Every day it's Hilton! He can't shoot and he can't pass and yet everyone says he's a great player just because he made All-America in football. I hope I get a chance at him this afternoon."

Lu Chung got his chance. Rockwell used the JV to present the Carlton attack, defense, and out-of-

TALENTED SOPHS   53

bounds plays. Then he described the strong and weak points of each of the Carlton players and demonstrated them with individual members of the JV squad. When he finished, Corrigan worked his regular starting five against Rockwell's squad and then they were excused. But Soapy moved up in the bleachers beside Murph Kelly to watch the varsity practice.

Down on the court, Corrigan was talking. "We'll have a thirty-minute scrimmage and call it a day. Starting team as is, and let's have Bollinger, Hilton, Di Santis, Tucker, and Slater out here to start."

The teams lined up and Lu Chung once again sought out and paired up against Chip. Soapy grunted in anticipation and nudged Kelly. "Watch this," he whispered. "Watch Chip."

"What's up?" Kelly asked.

"Just watch!"

Bollinger used last year's frosh jump signal and Chip came in high and got the tap and handed off to Tucker. Tucker hit Di Santis and the big fellow zipped the ball back to Chip in the backcourt. As soon as Chip caught the ball, Lu Chung dove forward and tried to knock the ball out of his hand. Then the little dribbler got a surprise. Chip jerked the ball back out of range and went around Lu Chung as if he were nailed to the floor.

Before one of Lu Chung's teammates could switch to cover him, Chip stopped at the head of the free-throw circle and used his jumper. The ball swished through the basket for the two-pointer without touching the rim.

Lu Chung was seething. "Lucky," he gritted. "Lucky shot."

Chip smiled and covered Lu Chung like a blanket,

and his opponent was forced to pass. And when Lu Chung reversed his direction, so he would be in position to regain the ball, Chip dropped carelessly back and turned his head to watch the ball.

Up in the bleachers, Soapy nudged Murph Kelly again. "Watch!"

"I'm watching!" Kelly growled. "Quit jabbing me!"

When Gowdy returned the pass, Chip erupted into action, intercepted the ball and was away with Lu Chung in swift pursuit. Chip drove under the basket and faked, and Lu Chung flew through the air in anticipation of the shot. At the last instant, Chip drew the ball back, watched Lu Chung fly past him and out of bounds, and then calmly reached up and banked the ball off the backboard and through the ring.

Jimmy took the ball out of bounds and passed it to Gowdy who brought the ball slowly upcourt. Jimmy could scarcely wait for the ball, but Gowdy passed to Markley and the co-captain hit Butcher King under the basket. The big senior hooked cleanly over Sky Bollinger's outstretched arm and the ball dropped through the hoop.

Sky caught the ball as it dropped through the cords and stepped back out of bounds. Then he rifled a pass to Rud Slater halfway up the court and Rud dribbled hard for the basket. But Markley cut him off and Rud passed back to Chip near the center of the court.

Chip held the ball at arm's length over his head and looped a high pass to Bollinger. Sky met the ball on the side of the lane and Chip ran Lu Chung into the block and cut through. But Butcher King saw the play coming and yelled, "Switch!" and picked Chip up as he drove past.

TALENTED SOPHS 55

Lu Chung switched back when Chip didn't get the ball and Bollinger dribbled to the corner. He held the ball until Chip maneuvered to a pivot position by the side of the basket, just outside the three-second lane. Then Sky gave Chip a perfect bounce pass. The rest was easy. Chip faked, drew the foul, and went right on up with the shot and scored. He tossed the free throw cleanly through the rim to complete the three-point play and dropped back on defense, feeling loose for the first time.

Lu Chung was wary now. And the next time Chip got the ball, the little fellow gave Chip plenty of room. Chip gauged the distance to the goal, faked a dribble, took a long step back, and let the ball fly. The set shot never touched the rim.

Soapy elbowed Murph Kelly nearly out of his seat. "You see that?" he demanded gleefully.

"I saw it, all right, and I like it," Kelly said, "but remember my age. I bruise easily. What fired Hilton up?"

"Lu Chung talked out of turn. Guess this will take care of *him*."

Kelly grinned. "Hope so. He had it coming."

After Chip's last shot, Corrigan substituted Speed Morris for Tucker and Bitsy Reardon for Chip. Then he moved Chip over to the varsity in place of Lu Chung. Chip had no difficulty blending in with the regulars, and following a short scrimmage, Corrigan excused the squad for the day.

Soapy made it back to the field house and dressed in nothing flat. And when Chip and Speed came out of Alumni Gym he was waiting, barely able to control his jubilation. "Nice going, Chipper. That was great!"

"It was a cheap thing to do," Chip said bitterly.

"Why?"

"Because it wasn't a fair match."

"But he asked for it, Chip. Look what he did to you! Where's the difference?"

"I thought we settled that Wednesday."

"You mean about me and Hong Kong?"

"That's right," Chip said shortly, "forget it."

About the same time, in another part of University, Jimmy Lu Chung was walking slowly toward one of the poorer sections of town where he rented a small, inexpensive room. He was in a thoughtful frame of mind, thoroughly mixed up about a lot of things. There was, first of all, his shaky position as a starting guard on the varsity; second, his poor play and removal from the game the previous night, and third, the emergence this afternoon of Chip Hilton as a dangerous competitor for his position.

Jimmy tried to tell himself that Hilton had been lucky that afternoon. But he knew deep in his heart that a fellow with Hilton's speed and passing and shooting ability, as demonstrated in the afternoon scrimmage, was no ordinary player. "Hip was right!" he muttered. "He's good. Now I *am* in the soup."

CHAPTER 7

BIG GUN FOR THE STATESMEN

HENRY ROCKWELL was only partly right about Carlton. The two teams were evenly matched with respect to height and both used the man-to-man defense, but there the comparison ended. Carlton's attack sparkled; State's offense sputtered. Corrigan started Markley, King, Thornhill, Gowdy, and Reb Tucker. And when this team failed to click, he began to experiment with different veteran combinations. This resulted in loss of confidence by the starters, as well as the reserve veterans, and the outcome was bad basketball. Carlton gradually forged ahead and led by a score of 42 to 30 at the half. The third period was a repetition of the first two, and it ended with Carlton still ahead by twelve points, 61 to 49.

Corrigan pulled all his veterans then and replaced them with Chip, Sky Bollinger, Speed Morris, Rud Slater, and Bitsy Reardon. "All right, fellows," he said, glancing at the scoreboard, "we're down twelve points, so we haven't got a thing to lose. Play them all over the court but watch the fouls. Another thing.

58   TOURNAMENT CRISIS

Switch on every cross. Got it? O.K., now go get 'em!"

The sophomores gave all they had and fought Carlton to a standstill. Their spirit and drive was so exciting after the dull play of the veterans that the State fans took heart and cheered them to the rafters. But it was too much to ask. The youngsters hadn't been together as a team since the previous year and Carlton had too much poise, lasted it out, and won by a score of 82 to 75.

By the time Chip and Speed finished dressing, it was too late to go to work and they walked slowly across the campus to Jeff. On the way, they got a milkshake and talked over the game.

"We nearly caught them," Speed said ruefully.

Chip nodded. "I've been thinking about that. You know, if we'd had Lu Chung in the game instead of Rud Slater we might have done it. He's fast, has wonderful reflexes, and loves a wide-open game. He's a natural for a press attack."

"You're right. I never thought of him that way."

"It wouldn't be bad," Chip continued. "Sky is big and fast, Bitsy is a flash of lightning, and you're as fast as they come. Hmmm."

"No one could say *you* had two left feet," Speed added. "I wish Corrigan would work us on it as a team."

"We can think about it and be ready the next time. Let's keep thinking about it. Well, I've got to get to bed. See you in the morning."

Down at State Drug, interest in the game had been high. Soapy kept dashing down the street to Pete's to catch a glimpse of the game on television and to find out whether or not Chip was in the game. The last time he appeared, Pete was raving.

"What's wrong with that coach? Why play all

GUN FOR THE STATESMEN 59

those stiffs when he's got a great player like Chip on the bench?"

Soapy didn't know the answer to that one. When he and Fireball and Whitty sauntered in after work, Pete's Place was jammed with customers.

"Be with you in a sec, Soapy!" Pete called. "Say, Chip got in the last quarter. Made sixteen points! Gray was talking about him on television. Now, what do you guys want? I gotta get some help in here. I'm bushed. Six hamburgers and three cups of what— Tea? Now I've heard everything! Hamburgers and tea!"

When Soapy got home, Chip was asleep and the redhead undressed quietly and went to bed. In the morning, he shook Chip awake.

"Locke is on Corrigan, Chip. Listen! Quote: 'Coach Jim Corrigan may have a veteran squad of basketball players but it is this reporter's understanding that the game of basketball is won by the team which puts the ball through the hoop more often than its opponents.

"'Last night at Alumni Gymnasium, Carlton won a dull contest by a score of 82 to 75, chiefly because the locals handled the ball as if it was an oversized egg and they were afraid to heave it at the basket, afraid it might break. This careful ball-handling was supposed to demonstrate Corrigan's famous possession passing attack, but its only effect on some thousands of fans was to send them away from the game with little to remember about a wasted evening except that they had been firsthand witnesses to a first-class sports bust.

"'The only spark of life was provided by Chip Hilton, a sophomore up from last year's frosh team, who scored sixteen points during the ten minutes he was in the game. Hilton averaged thirty-four points per game as a freshman and that probably is the reason Corrigan kept him on the bench. . . .'

"And listen to this, Chip. 'Southwestern won its thirty-ninth straight game last night. As usual, it was Bordon and Rip Ralk who led the way. Bordon under the basket with his sensational hooks and tap-ins, and Ralk with his set shots and driving jump shots.'"

"Thirty-nine in a row," Chip said admiringly. "What a record! I'd be proud just to sit the bench on a team like that."

"Don't worry, you'd have a starting spot. C'mon. I'm starved."

After breakfast, Chip and Soapy hustled down to State Drug and worked steadily through the day. Chip was thinking ahead to the game that night and the hours slipped away like minutes. Then he was in the dressing room and Corrigan was giving his pregame talk.

"We learned a lot last night and I know we're not going to let Carlton beat us two nights in succession. Let's go out there and play *real* basketball."

State did all right, jumped into the lead after a ragged start by both teams, and remained out in front during the entire game. Chip got a chance in the second and fourth quarters and was sensational, scoring twenty-nine points and bringing the fans to their feet time after time with his accurate shooting.

"You see that? You see that shot?"

"They can't hold him! I never saw anything like it!"

"How can Corrigan keep *him* off the team?"

Jimmy Lu Chung was bitterly disappointed and it showed in his behavior on the bench. He groused

GUN FOR THE STATESMEN 61

and sat with folded arms, never once joining his bench teammates in cheering a good play on the court. Corrigan seemed to have forgotten all about the dribbling wizard and did not give him a chance until there was only three minutes left to play.

As soon as he was in the game and the first time he got his hands on the ball, Lu Chung dribbled in for a shot. Chip followed in, got the ball, passed it back to Lu Chung, and maneuvered his opponent into a pick. When he broke for the basket, there was six feet of daylight between himself and his guard, but Lu Chung passed him up and held the ball. Before there was time for another shot, the game was over.

The dressing room was full of chatter and horseplay but Lu Chung did not join in the fun. He was still upset and banged his shoes and suit into the locker and slammed the door. On the way out of the building, Chip found himself beside Lu Chung and tried to cheer him up. "Don't worry about it, Jimmy. You'll be back in there. Coach is just trying everyone out."

Lu Chung shrugged his shoulders and glared at Chip without a word. At the first corner he turned off and strode away without answering Chip's good night. A few minutes later he was in his usual hangout, a little restaurant off the campus in the poorer section of University, where George Long, one of his school friends worked.

"What happened?" Long asked, gesturing toward the television set on the wall. "Why didn't you play?"

Jimmy threw himself down on a chair. "Too many big-shot football stars out for the team."

"That fellow Hilton was terrific. Got twenty-nine points. High scorer of the game."

"I hate the guy," Lu Chung said angrily. "The jerk!" Then, noting the expression on Long's face, he reflected a second and continued lamely, "Maybe I don't hate him but— Aw, heck, I don't know how I feel about him."

"I know how *I* feel about him!"

Lu Chung was surprised. "You know him?"

"Not personally, but I know him well enough to tell you that you're wrong about the jerk business. He's anything *but!* I happen to know! And no matter how *you* feel about his basketball ability, Jimmy, he's going to be the star of the team."

"What do you mean, you know him?"

"I know he's a gentleman. Have you ever been in Pete's Place? That little restaurant on Tenth Street?"

"Don't think so. Why?"

"Well, I went in there for a cup of tea the other night and some fellows were sitting in a booth talking basketball. Naturally, knowing you, I listened in. Then Hilton and a fellow by the name of Soapy came in and one of the fellows in the booth spoke to this Soapy and said he was glad he'd been cut from the squad because he didn't care to play on the same team with a foreigner . . ."

Lu Chung shook his head. "I don't get it."

"He meant you," Long continued. "He called you by name."

"But I'm no foreigner. I'm a Chinese-American. But what's that got to do with Hilton?"

"Plenty! Hilton told him off! He said you were born of naturalized parents and were as much a citizen or an American as he or anyone else. Hilton really shut him up!"

"You're not kidding? He really did that? Stood up for me?"

GUN FOR THE STATESMEN 63

"He sure did."

There was a short, tense silence. Then Lu Chung struck the table with his fist, jarring the cups and spilling the tea. "I'm a jerk," he said disgustedly. "I wonder when I'll really grow up. I've sure been wrong about him." He reflected a moment, nodding his head thoughtfully. Then he eyed his friend steadily and continued, "You're right about the basketball part of it, too, George. He *is* a great player."

After Lu Chung turned off, Chip continued to State Drug and a few minutes later joined Soapy, Fireball, and Whitty at Pete's restaurant. Pete greeted Chip warmly. "What happened to you last night? Missed you. You hear what Gee-Gee Gray had to say about you on his sportscast? Your ears burn last night?"

Chip grinned. "Nope, but maybe that's why I had some bad dreams."

"Uh, uh. It was all good. You stick around—it will be better tonight. Speakin' of bad dreams, I was so tired last night when I got to bed I couldn't even sleep. This place has been mobbed for the past week."

Soapy elbowed Chip. "Why don't you break down and hire some help?" he gibed.

"You ever try hiring restaurant help? They last about a week and they're gone and you look again. Seriously, though, if you run across someone who wants a job, send him around. But he's gotta have experience. Ain't got time to teach a guy how to carry a glass of water without spilling it."

Chip's pals wanted to know all about the game and he had to replay it for them. He was glad when they reached Jeff and he could get to bed. He was always dead tired when Sunday rolled around and he looked forward to a good, long, late sleep.

But not Soapy Smith. Soapy was always wide awake at the crack of dawn. And Sunday was no exception. He slipped quietly out of the room and went for the papers. Chip was half awake when Soapy returned, but that meant little to Soapy. He yanked the paper open to the sports page and sat down on his bed.

"Listen to this, Chip. Quote: 'After two straight defeats, State got into the winning column last night at Alumni Gym, defeating Carlton 79 to 64 to break even in the two-game series.

"'Chip Hilton proved to be the big gun for the Statesmen, scoring twenty-nine points in twenty minutes of play . . .'"

"All right, I know. I was there, remember?"

"O.K., how about this? Quote: 'Southwestern won its fortieth consecutive victory last night and appeared unbeatable. Coach Jeff Habley's N.C.A.A. and Holiday Invitational Champions brushed aside Southern Poly, 109–64, with All-America "Two-Ton" Tom Bordon scoring thirty-two points and hogging twenty-six rebounds, while his teammate, All-America Ralph "Rip" Ralk, scored twenty-nine points during the eighteen minutes he saw action . . .' Wow, Chip! How about those guys?"

"Fabulous, that's all. Well, I suppose you're happy now that you've got me wide awake. But remember this— When I get back from church, I'm going to take a long nap. Then I'm going to study. All day! Understand?"

"Have no fears, my famous pal. I've got a little errand which concerns Miss Mitzi Savrill and it will

GUN FOR THE STATESMEN 65

keep me busy all day, starting as of now. See you for lunch."

Chip dressed leisurely, ate a light breakfast at a small restaurant just off the campus, and started for church. He had taken less than ten steps when he passed a young fellow, slouching along with his head lowered and his hands thrust deep in his pockets, evidently steeped in thought. Chip glanced at the walker and was surprised to see that it was Jimmy Lu Chung.

"Hi, Lu Chung. Going anywhere in particular?"

Lu Chung, startled out of his reverie, jumped. He recovered his poise quickly and shook his head. "Why, no, Hilton. Just taking a walk."

"If you're not doing anything, how about going along to church with me?"

Jimmy was surprised. His eyes opened a bit wider, and he stared questioningly at Chip. "Why, sure. That would be swell." He paused and looked at his clothes. "I—"

"You look all right. Come on."

They matched strides for a few steps, each a little uncomfortable. Lu Chung was the first to speak. "You know something, Hilton?"

"Call me Chip."

"Chip, then— You're the first fellow on the squad who has really been friendly. And I've been too much of a chump to realize it."

"Why, they think you're great, Jimmy!"

"No, it's something else. They laugh at me but they don't really like me. I guess it's because I'm such a show-off."

"You're wrong. Everyone likes you. Well, here we are."

Chip and Jimmy sat quietly through the church

service, and an hour later when they walked slowly down the steps with the other worshipers, each realized he had found a friend.

"What did you think of the sermon?" Chip asked.

"We worship a little differently, Chip, but I thought it was swell. All the time the minister was talking, I was thinking about sports. Seems to me sportsmanship in almost anything a fellow does is on the religious side."

"No doubt about it, Jimmy. The Golden Rule just about covers everything: 'Do unto others as you would have others do unto you.'"

Jimmy nodded. "Yes," he agreed thoughtfully. "That *would* cover about everything."

They continued along in silence and then Chip put his thoughts into words. "Jimmy, I'd like to be your friend and I'd like you to be my friend. But there's something wrong—"

"Nothing is wrong, Chip," Jimmy said slowly. "Nothing but me. I love basketball and my heart is set on making the team. It means more to me right now than anything else in the world, almost . . ." He shrugged and spread his hands. "I guess I might just as well say it—I was trying to show you up because I was afraid you would beat me out for the team.

"I'm from Clinton, Chip, and I've been hoping I could start against Wilson Tech in my home town. We go out there on the fifteenth and if I can play in that game—why, everything in my little world will be tops. That is except—"

"Except what?"

"Well, I've just got to have a job and quick. I've been hoping I could hang on this semester."

"I thought you were on the G.I. Bill of Rights."

Jimmy Lu Chung stared questioningly at Chip

"I am. But unfortunately, every penny I can spare has to go home to help the family. Right now, things are pretty serious with my pop's business."

"What sort of work are you looking for?"

"Any kind of work. Manual labor or restaurant— Guess I ought to know the restaurant business," Jimmy said glumly. "I've worked in one just about all my life. That's our business in Clinton." His voice grew tight. "Not that there's much business—"

Chip stopped short and snapped his fingers. "I've got it! I know where you can get a job. What are you doing tomorrow after practice?"

"Nothing. That's the trouble."

"Good. I've got an idea and I'm going to put it to work right now. I'll tell you about it tomorrow at practice."

CHAPTER 8

FIVE PLAYERS ALL THE WAY

CHIP headed straight for Pete's Place, his spirits high and his long legs eating up the distance. Soapy was absorbed with a crossword puzzle in one of the booths which lined the wall opposite the counter and Chip slid into the seat opposite his pal.

"English assignment?"

Soapy shook his head. "Naw," he growled, "just trying to win a trip to China! Wanta learn how to dribble a basketball!"

"Now, Soapy—"

"I was just kidding." Soapy grinned disarmingly and winked at Pete who had approached the booth. "Gimme a hot dog and a milkshake, eh, Pete?"

Pete grimaced. "It's your stomach—" He leaned against the side of the booth and turned to Chip. "What can I do *you* for, Chip?"

"Oh, a cheese sandwich and a glass of milk, I guess. Say, Pete, that job you spoke about still open?"

"Sure is. Know someone who can fill the bill?"

"I think so. He's had restaurant experience and he needs a job."

"A student?"

"Yes. Chinese-American and a fine fellow."

Soapy's head shot up and he looked at Chip in astonishment. "Chinese-American," he repeated.

"How about the language?" Pete asked.

"Speaks better English than either of us."

Pete hesitated. "Don't know, Chip. Some pretty rough guys hang out in here." His quick glance caught the disappointment in Chip's eyes and he added quickly, "But for you—anything! Bring him around."

"There's one more thing, Pete. He's a great basketball player and he's on the team."

Pete's face lit up. "He is? Now that puts a different light on it!" He eyed Chip keenly, nodding his head understandingly. "Uh, *huh!* And you want me to fix it so he can practice and play the games. That's easy enough! Fact is, it oughta help business. Fancy me, having a varsity basketball player working in the joint. Sure he can get off. Any time!"

When Chip and Soapy finished eating, Pete marked the amount of their tabs in the little black book on the cash register and advised Chip that he would be expecting his new employee the next afternoon. "Thanks, Chip," he said appreciatively. "And don't worry. I'll treat him right."

Once outside Pete's Place, Soapy could restrain his curiosity no longer. "What's that all about? Why a job for Lu Chung?"

"Because he needs work."

"How do you know?"

Chip told Soapy about taking Jimmy to church and their understanding. "He's all right, Soapy. He's lonesome and he needs friends. From what I could gather, Jimmy feels he is disliked."

Soapy grunted. "He's so right! What an attitude! I hope all Chinese-Americans aren't show-offs like

FIVE PLAYERS 71

him. Hey, you've been studying Chinese history in that course with Prof Haskins. Are all the Chinese like Lu Chung?"

"If you mean show-offs, of course not. But Chinese *are* great showmen. You'll have to admit Jimmy is clever."

"He's clever, all right. Especially when it comes to dribbling."

"He paid a price for that, Soapy. The Chinese have a lot of perseverance. Prof Haskins keeps pounding that into us. One of his favorite Chinese axioms is: 'The sea was great; the bird small. The bird picked up stones and dropped them into the sea until the sea was filled.'"

"All right, they're persevering. So what?"

"They're more than that—they're strong and intense and they never give up. They've lost wars, too, but the Chinese have never surrendered their souls or ideals."

"All right," Soapy agreed grudgingly, "they're clever and persevering and strong and have high ideals. I hope all this means your new pal will do an about-face and try to be a regular guy."

"He will. Come on. I've got to hit the books."

Monday's papers played up the coming game at Southwestern on Wednesday night. But it was all Southwestern. The writers cited all sorts of statistics covering the forty-game winning streak and the twin championships of the previous season; the Holiday Invitational Tournament and the N.C.A.A. Championship. Yet, with all the coverage by the sports writers, Henry Rockwell gave State's varsity some inside dope on Southwestern that could scarcely have been provided by Coach Jeff Habley himself.

Rockwell had his JV team all set by the time the

varsity appeared and plunged right into his scouting notes. As he explained the type of attack and defense the great team used, the JV players demonstrated the moves on the court. Then Rockwell discussed each Southwestern player in detail.

"Bordon averages around thirty points a game. He's listed as six-eleven, but it's my guess he's seven feet in height or better. Don't be fooled by his weight. The program says he weighs two hundred and sixty pounds and I believe it. He isn't called Two-Ton for nothing. But that doesn't mean he can't use it. He's strong and rough and he's been around . . .

"Watch his elbows, you centers. He's extremely liberal and will let you have one any time."

That brought a laugh but it died away as the players caught the grim undercurrent in Rockwell's voice.

"Bordon is good. But if I were asked to choose their key player it would have to be Rip Ralk. Ralk is six-four, weighs about two-ten, and is good for twenty-five or thirty points a game. He scores chiefly on tip-in plays and jumpers, and he's always up on the boards. Now this may sound impossible, but it's another tribute to his greatness. He's smart enough and fast enough to cover the boards and still direct the attack and the defense.

"The other big man is Perkins. He plays the corners on the offense and sets the picks and blocks for the cutters. On the defense he plays the opponents' second big man."

A brief smile whisked across Rockwell's lips as he continued. "At the guard positions they have a couple of little fellows: Jim Lloyd and Joe Munn. Lloyd is six-two, a hundred and eighty-five pounds, and gets about ten points a game. Munn is about

FIVE PLAYERS

the same size. They're both steady players and make few mistakes.

"Coach Jeff Habley plays those five players all the way. Not that he hasn't got good reserves, but Habley believes his starting five should carry the load.

"Now, I hesitate to say this, but Coach Corrigan and I both think it is only fair: Southwestern plays rough, tough, and what I would call, unnecessarily bruising basketball. The players throw their elbows around carelessly and are expert at double-teaming an opposing rebounder with the kind of body contact which—er—shall I say—leaves a memory?

"The three big men are especially expert in the use of their hips when you try to drive through and you can expect a shove in the back if you're in the way. Oh, yes. I might add that they are exceptionally clever. You've all heard about legendary officials with eyes in the back of their heads. Well," Rockwell paused and continued dryly, "they wouldn't be good enough!"

After Rockwell finished his notes, Corrigan scrimmaged the squad right through the full hour which remained. Chip and Jimmy dressed quickly and hurried down to Pete's Place. After the introductions, Pete put Jimmy right to work.

Soapy was behind the fountain when Chip came in through the Tenth Street entrance. "All right?" he asked.

Chip nodded. "Already on the job."

The evening rush tapered off at nine o'clock, and Chip slipped out the side door and down the block to Pete's Place. Pete was serving coffee to one of the customers who sat at the counter, but Jimmy was not in sight. When Pete finished with the customer, he hurried up to Chip, his face wreathed in smiles.

"Lookin' for Jimmy? He's in the kitchen. Know what he's doin'? He's cleanin' up the place. You could eat off the floor in the kitchen. Boy, can that kid work! He's a human dynamo. Heck, he's better on a quick order than the chef himself."

"The customers like him?"

"Like him? They think he's great. He's got 'em practically eating out of his hand."

"Tell him I'll be back after work."

"Right, Chip. He'll be here."

Soapy and Fireball and Whitty had no curfew responsibilities and could take their time after work, but not Chip and Jimmy. Chip watched the clock and started for Pete's Place just before closing time. Jimmy was waiting and they walked slowly up the street.

"Oh, boy," Jimmy groaned, "am I tired!"

"How did it go?"

"Fine, Chip. I like to be on the go, and Pete's Place sure fills that need. I wish Pop's restaurant was that busy. Maybe I wouldn't have to worry."

"What's wrong with your father's restaurant?"

Jimmy appeared reluctant to talk about it at first, but after a few steps he began. From his talk, Chip sensed that Jimmy was disturbed by the fact that his father had never discarded his old-country customs and had never modernized the restaurant or its service. "Pop tries to run the business as if he were still in China. He can't seem to understand that the customers want service and modern surroundings."

"Lots of Americans like foreign-type restaurants, Jimmy."

"I know, Chip, but our restaurant is practically

on the Tech campus, and to begin with, it isn't that kind of restaurant. Pop could make a fortune if he served American food and gave his customers real service . . .

"That's the reason my brother Tommy left. He didn't think it made sense to keep the restaurant open all day when there were no customers, and then try to make ends meet by serving tea and expensive dishes at night to twenty or thirty people. Especially when it meant losing money."

"What's Tommy doing now?"

Jimmy grinned. "Just what you would expect. Working in an American restaurant in Chicago."

"You and Tommy seem to think alike. Couldn't you team up and change your father's point of view?"

"No, Chip, you don't understand. In our way of life, the eldest son"—Jimmy paused and tapped his chest—"that's me— The eldest son is treated like a man and has to follow his father's orders to the letter. His father never shows affection for him and it's tough. Especially when you've grown up in America and your father keeps stressing the virtues—

"You call them responsibilities. *Your* responsibilities to *your* family—and to *your* laws and customs —are something like ours, with the exception that the eldest son of a Chinese family is trained from infancy to observe them to the letter. I've always tried to do that, Chip, out of reverence to my father."

"I think that's fine."

"It is, up to a certain point. But Pop is always talking about going back to China, and how vital and important it is to us. But I feel that I am an American and I *never* want to go back to China.

"You see, the old Chinese feel that the village of their birth is the most beloved spot on earth and consider it a disgrace to die any place except in their original home town."

"Has your father been back to China?"

"Sure, years ago. You see, my grandpop sent Pop over here as a student, but he didn't have enough money and had to go to work. Anyway, he saved his money and went back home to China and married my mother and brought her here. Pop plans to go back to the old country when we've saved enough money."

"But you're an American and your whole family are Americans. Why go back?"

"All the old people want to go back, Chip. They just can't believe that anything over there is changed." Jimmy shook his head firmly. "I never want to leave America. I love this country and I want to live here until I die."

"Well, you can, can't you?"

"Yes and no. It's hard to explain. I'm a Chinese-American, Chip. But loyalty to the family is a matter of honor. I love my family with all my heart and obedience to one's elders is one of our most precious beliefs. That's where the responsibilities of an American boy differ from the virtues as practiced by a Chinese boy. Guess you've been reading all that in your Chinese history class. At any rate, it's a matter of obedience. So—"

"How many in the family, Jimmy?"

Jimmy counted on his fingers. "There's my mother, and Tommy—he's twenty years old—the four girls, my father, and my grandfather. My grandfather is old and not very active in things. But my pop tries to make the whole family think *his* way and it just won't work. Tommy thinks American, period! So . . . he's in Chicago and Pop never even mentions his name. But, as you know, I'm the eldest son—and, well, I must do as Pop says."

"Maybe everything will change when you get out of college, Jimmy," Chip said. "You'll be older and able to do a lot of things for your family."

"I hope you're right," Jimmy said softly. "Well, here's where I turn off and I guess I'd better go home. I'm tired out. Good night, Chip, and thanks for the job and everything . . ."

Practice the next day continued where it had left off the previous afternoon. Rockwell and his JV squad again demonstrated the kind of basketball State could expect at Southwestern, and Corrigan put them through another fast scrimmage. When Chip and Jimmy came out of the gym, they found Soapy waiting.

Jimmy had been fully cognizant of Soapy's feelings toward him and was immediately on guard. But it wasn't necessary. The new Jimmy Lu Chung was good enough for Soapy Smith. If Chip thought Jimmy was all right, Soapy thought he was all right.

"Well, now that you know what you're going to be up against, what are you planning to do about it?" Soapy demanded.

"Take it as it comes and try to win," Chip said.

"Well, you better get a good rest on that train. You're in for a rough time tomorrow night."

Jimmy was doubtful. "They couldn't play that way and get away with it, could they?"

"Yes, sir!" Soapy said convincingly. "If Rock says they play that kind of basketball, that's the way they play!"

CHAPTER 9

HOW GENTLEMEN PLAY THE GAME

SOUTHWESTERN looked just like any other medium-sized city from the train window. The first evidences pointing to the approach to a city were the small farms, scattered houses, residential areas, and the usual industrial buildings; mammoth plants and a number of small factories, and railroad yards and tracks lined with long rows of freight cars. The station, too, was like any other railroad terminal.

State's varsity basketball players had lost interest in the scenery long ago. It was midday, and they were interested only in chow. "When do we eat?" they cried, grabbing their suitcases and uniform bags and spilling out on the platform. Then the "treatment" began. . . .

First it was a newsboy, holding an armful of papers and pointing to the front page. "Get your papers here, gents. Read all about it! Read all about the big game!"

Butcher King loomed up above him and reached for a paper and recognition dawned. "Hey! You guys from State? Well, take my advice! Get back on the train!"

Chip glanced at the streamer which stretched across the top of the page in big block letters.

SOUTHWESTERN SEEKS VICTORY
NUMBER 41

"Front-page headline!" Jimmy exclaimed unbelievingly. "Just like a war!"

They barged on through the waiting room and out to a line of taxicabs. Markley, Thornhill, Jimmy, and Chip piled into one and the driver stepped on the gas. Then they got some more of the "treatment."

"You fellows like to window-shop? Take a look!" The driver pointed. Every store along the street had a big 41 painted on the windows.

"*Now* I've seen everything!" Jimmy said.

The campus was hoop crazy, too. The students on the walks stopped and stared and greeted them with good-natured hoots and jeers. It was no different in the lobby of the Campus Hotel. Signs covered the walls offering all manner of advice to the "victims."

"Take it serious, don't they?" Markley observed.

"And how!" Thornhill said shortly.

They rested after lunch, and then Corrigan took them over to the new Southwestern field house for shooting practice. State's Alumni Gymnasium was beautiful but it couldn't compare with this elaborate structure. The giant lobby seemed as big as a football field, and was lined with row upon row of trophy cases containing hundreds of stuffed game balls and sparkling cups.

Chip walked through a lobby door and found himself on the mezzanine above the basketball court. He walked down to one of the boxes and viewed the glittering court below. It looked almost like a painting. "It's beautiful," he murmured aloud.

"You can say that again," someone behind him agreed.

As soon as Chip turned, he knew the middle-aged man who extended his hand was a sports writer.

"Hello, Hilton. My name's Gary. Bill Gary of the *Chronicle*. Recognized you from your picture. Ran it in the paper today. You like our court, eh?"

"I've never seen anything like it."

"You've never seen anything like our team, either. We've got some of the greatest players the game has ever seen." He appraised Chip's broad, sloping shoulders and big hands. "You must be pretty good yourself. Unusual for a sophomore football player to crash varsity basketball."

"I guess you could call it luck."

"That isn't what I hear. Come along. I'll walk you down to the dressing room."

Gary knew Corrigan and stopped to chat with him, and Chip joined his teammates and slipped into his uniform. When he walked out on the highly polished floor, he found himself on tiptoe, stepping gingerly, as though he was walking on the top of a mirror. Corrigan held shooting practice for half an hour and then excused everyone, advising them that the pregame meal would be served at four o'clock sharp.

Chip and Jimmy walked back to the hotel and relaxed in the lobby with the papers. Chip opened the *Chronicle* to the sports page and more of the "treatment" jumped out at him.

LOCALS READY FOR VICTIM 41
Visitors to Start Football Star

State arrived in town to meet Southwestern's National Basketball Champions tonight at the SW field house and

GENTLEMEN PLAY THE GAME 81

are slated to be victim number 41. The visitors lost their first two games but bounced back against Carlton last Saturday night to break into the victory column by a score of 79 to 64.

Chip Hilton, National A.A.U. Basketball Marksmanship Champion and State's All-American sophomore football quarterback star, scored 29 points against Carlton and is expected to spearhead the attack of the Statesmen against SW tonight.

Probable Starting Line-ups

	Southwestern				*State*		
F	Ralk	44 Sr.	6–4	F	Markley	63 Sr.	6–3
F	Perkins	55 Sr.	6–6	F	Thornhill	86 Sr.	5–11
C	Bordon	33 Sr.	6–11	C	King	94 Jr.	6–9
G	Lloyd	66 Jr.	6–2	G	Hilton	44 Soph.	6–2
G	Munn	77 Sr.	6–3	G	Gowdy	75 Sr.	6–1

Chip glanced quickly at Jimmy who was sitting nearby and then folded the paper. "How about a walk?" he suggested. "Let's take a look at the campus."

It was four o'clock when they returned, and after eating, Corrigan took them for a brisk walk and then put them to bed. Chip couldn't sleep, but he and Jimmy and Speed rested and talked a bit about the Southwestern team.

A preliminary game was in progress when State arrived at the field house that night and they watched the action until the end of the half. When they left to suit up, every seat in the big arena was filled.

Corrigan wasted no time on a pregame pep talk. The treatment had taken care of him and the players as well. He merely joined in the team clasp and said, "Give 'em all you've got!"

Chip followed Markley and Thornhill in the line

of players and expected to hear a round of welcoming applause from the fans when they ran out on the floor. But there was hardly a sound. State went right into the usual warm-up, each player feeling a bit angry at the continuance of the treatment which had dogged them every step since arrival at the railroad station.

Then, without warning, they got another dose. A siren shrilled and wailed piercingly through the great arena and the murmuring crowd noise died away until the only sound was the padding feet of the State players and the thump of the ball. Then the lights flickered out.

Surprised by the darkness and the strange silence of the crowd, Chip and his teammates looked around at the pale circle of faces. "What goes?" King growled.

"Got me," Thornhill said. "What are they so quiet about?"

"Another trick," Markley said cynically.

It was a trick, all right. But it was showmanship, too. For five large orange circles, each with a huge 41 in the center, began to glow under the Southwestern basket.

The brilliant circles grew brighter and brighter, and then, in company with a tremendous explosion, the lights flashed on and Southwestern's five starters, each carrying a ball, broke through the circles. The band broke into a strident march and the crowd went mad.

Chip and his State teammates were wholly unprepared and could only stand and stare as Bordon and Ralk and Perkins and Lloyd and Munn each dribbled hard for the basket and dunked his ball cleanly through the hoop. Then the remaining members of

GENTLEMEN PLAY THE GAME 83

the Southwestern squad joined in and every player dunked the ball, drawing a tremendous cheer each time. That was the treatment's grand finale and in a few minutes the real business of the evening was under way.

Chip got a quick introduction to the Southwestern playing techniques. He lined up against Rip Ralk and the big fellow gave Chip a quick, hard handclasp. Then Ralk turned away without a word. But when the ball left the official's hand for the center jump, he turned and nearly knocked Chip to the floor as he drove high in the air for the ball. Chip recovered quickly and shot a quick glance at the official, but there was no whistle.

That first play set the pattern. Southwestern moved the ball until Bordon or Ralk got a good shot. Then Perkins joined in and the three of them pounded the board, following the shot if it was unsuccessful and tapping the ball up and up and up again until it fell through the hoop.

The champions played a tight man-to-man defense, each player picking up his assigned opponent at the ten-second line and sticking to him like glue. When a State player tried to drive through, he always ran into an elbow. If he succeeded in getting ahead of his opponent, a clutching hand checked him. Although the officials called a few of the fouls, they were few and far between and the result was alley basketball. Almost anything short of a knockdown was overlooked.

But it was effective! And it stopped Corrigan's four-man weave before it could get started. State's attack degenerated into a mad scramble. It was every man for himself. The Southwestern players were openly contemptuous of State's efforts and kept up a derisive chatter. And if the purpose behind the display of poor sportsmanship was to upset their opponents, it was highly successful.

Chip was indignant, filled with bitterness. The "treatment" had been humiliating, but this was worse. He forgot all about blending in with the veterans and concentrated on trying to beat Southwestern all by himself. Never before had Chip forgotten the importance of team play; now he concentrated on putting the ball through the hoop at every opportunity. On the defense he gave Ralk as good as he received. Several times he stole the ball away and dribbled the length of the court for a score.

The Southwestern fans were unfriendly but they were, after all, rabid basketball fans. They had seldom seen an individual performance to match Chip's perfect play and their applause, modest at first, gradually increased with each brilliant play. But Chip couldn't do it all, and despite his sixteen points, Southwestern led at the half: 39 to 29.

Corrigan was the last to reach the dressing room and the expression clouding his face clearly expressed his feelings. "This is disgraceful!" he raged. "In all my years as a player and as a coach I have never seen anything like it. . . .

"For two cents I'd tell you to dress and we'd pull out of here right now! But that, they'd like! No, I won't put myself in their class. We'll fight it out! And we'll keep our heads and show them all—coach, team, fans, and everyone else—how gentlemen play the game. Sportsmanship? They don't know the meaning of the word!

"All right, I guess I haven't been much help. But there isn't much I can tell you to do against this kind of basketball . . . Officiating either! But we'll play clean if it kills us. That will hurt them more than a whipping."

Chip had never felt so anxious to play. When the teams lined up for the center tap to start the second half, Chip played dummy, and watched Ralk out of the corner of his eye. The official tossed up the ball and Ralk tried to repeat his first trick. But Chip beat him to it, took off a split second before the big All-American got started, and got the ball. Before Ralk landed, Chip had started his dribble.

Ralk twisted around and followed Chip clear to the goal and tried to stop the shot, but Chip released the ball with his inside hand and Ralk hacked the wrong arm. This time the foul was right out in the open for everyone to see, impossible to miss, and impossible to overlook. The ball swished through the net just as the referee blasted his whistle.

Chip toed the free-throw line and dropped the ball cleanly through the basket and the three-point play made the score: Southwestern 39, State 32.

Lloyd and Munn brought the ball upcourt and passed to Ralk. He passed to Bordon on the pivot and King blocked the big fellow's shot with a tremendous leap. Markley drifted back, got the ball, and fired it to Chip on the side line halfway up the court. Before Ralk could reach him, Chip dribbled downcourt, along the base line and around under the basket. He faked the hook shot, and when Ralk left his feet, Chip pivoted back and calmly banked the ball against the backboard and into the basket for the two-pointer.

"My, my," Markley said. "Did you see that? An All-American leaving his feet on the defense."

It was a beautiful play, and hostile as they were, the fans paid tribute with a round of applause.

86 TOURNAMENT CRISIS

Ralk was boiling. He grabbed the ball, stepped out of bounds, and passed to Munn. Or tried to pass! Chip timed it just right, pivoted toward Munn, and caught the ball. One long step and he dropped the

The charge sent Chip flying feet-

GENTLEMEN PLAY THE GAME 87

ball through the hoop. That made the score: Southwestern 39, State 36, and the fans were in a frenzy. Southwestern hadn't scored a point in the second half.

Munn took the ball out of bounds this time and Chip leeched on to Ralk, dogging him every step up the court. Bordon and Perkins tried to help Ralk, broke out behind Chip, and set up a double block. It worked! Ralk cut for the basket and Chip was trapped. He couldn't get through or around Bordon and Perkins, so he took a chance and broke for the State basket.

Just as if it had been rehearsed, Butcher King dropped back. And when Munn floated a soft pass over the heads of Bordon and Perkins toward Ralk,

first into the padded support

Butcher leaped high in the air and batted the ball far downcourt toward the State goal. Ralk saw King leap, and turned and sprinted after Chip.

Chip had guessed right and was right on top of the ball. He caught up to the ball on its first bounce and continued on with a hard dribble straight for the goal. He was out in front all alone and in the clear. Behind him, Ralk was sprinting toward the State goal for all he was worth. Chip took off at the circle and seemed to float toward the basket through the air.

Just as he released the ball for the lay-up shot over the front rim, Ralk made a desperate leap over Chip's shoulder and tried to hit the ball. But he was too late and the momentum of his charge carried him into Chip's back. The charge sent Chip flying feet-first into the padded support behind the basket. But the shot was perfect, cleared the rim, and Chip saw it bob through the net. Then he heard the official's whistle blast for the foul.

Chip grinned and scrambled to his knees. Then he felt the pain. He got to his feet and made a step and found that his right leg couldn't support his weight. He took another step toward the free-throw line and stopped. He couldn't walk. . . .

CHAPTER 10

A LESSON IN SPORTSMANSHIP

MURPHY KELLY was off the bench and out on the floor before the official got the whistle out of his mouth. As Chip stood there, swaying on his one good leg, the turmoil of the crowd quieted just as it had before the game. Chip's teammates circled anxiously around him, ominously silent while Kelly examined the knee. "Don't try to stand on it, Chip," Kelly said sharply. "Here, Morris, make a handseat with me."

Kelly and Speed carried Chip to the side line and through the aisle leading to the State dressing room. Then, almost as if ashamed of their conduct, the crowd began to applaud. As the trio disappeared from view, the applause reached a voluminous thunder and continued unabated until play had been resumed on the floor.

Corrigan was furiously angry. He followed Chip and Kelly and Speed clear to the end of the floor, and as he walked back in front of the Southwestern bench, it was obvious that he was restraining his temper with difficulty. He gave Jeff Habley a long, fierce look before continuing to his own bench where the State squad was grouped close together, glaring angrily at the Southwestern players.

"Skip it!" he ordered shortly. "Don't lose your heads. Remember, we're trying to give these people a lesson in sportsmanship. . . .

"All right, Jimmy, in for Chip. You'll have to shoot the foul."

Jimmy was trembling with ill-suppressed fury. His jaw was set in a grim line, and his light-brown eyes were flashing dangerously. Without a word he turned and dashed out on the floor.

"Jimmy!" Corrigan yelled. "Report!"

Jimmy turned back toward the scoring table and the man at the book acknowledged the intent and waved him into the game. The referee nodded and handed Jimmy the ball and the little fighter walked to the free-throw line. He bounced the ball to gain time and then took the shot, and the ball swished through the net to tie the score: Southwestern 39, State 39.

Southwestern's Bordon caught the ball as it cleared the net and he stepped quickly out of bounds. Then he passed to Stuff Lloyd in the corner and the fleet guard dribbled quickly upcourt. Jimmy picked Ralk up at the ten-second line and stuck with him like a postage stamp. The big fellow contemptuously ignored Jimmy, relaxed, and then suddenly cut for the basket, trying to pick Jimmy off on the high post which Bordon had set up on the free-throw line. But Jimmy was too fast, he darted between the two giants and covered Ralk like a blanket.

Butcher King, at six-nine, was two inches shorter than Bordon. But he had the weight to match the big All-America star's mad rushes and he was giving Two-Ton as good as he received. King saw the play coming and dropped back to make the switch. But when he saw Jimmy wouldn't need help, he

LESSON IN SPORTSMANSHIP 91

grinned appreciatively. "Nice going, Jimmy!" he called. "Stay! Stay!"

"Attaboy, Jimmy," Markley called encouragingly. "Stick with him!"

Ralk didn't like the taunt in Markley's voice and tried one of his tricks. He slowed down, yawned, and glanced at a spectator on the side line. Then Rip suddenly stepped on the gas and tried to outrace Jimmy to the basket. The change-of-pace trick was good but not fast enough, and Ralk was surprised to find Jimmy right in his path.

Ralk could have stopped or changed direction but he didn't even try; he mouthed something angrily and crashed into and over the little fellow, knocking him to the floor: It was a deliberate charging foul and obvious to everyone.

The referee blasted his whistle and stooped to help Jimmy to his feet. "You all right, fellow?" he asked solicitously.

Markley lost his head and charged toward Ralk. "That was a dirty trick!" he cried. "What are you trying to do?"

Both benches had emptied and players from both teams were edging out on the floor. The referee blasted his whistle again and dashed between Markley and Ralk. "Cut it out, you two," he threatened, "or out you go!" He turned toward the benches flanking the scoring table. "You sit down, too!" he stormed. "All of you! Get off the floor! What is this?"

Meanwhile, Jimmy had reached the free-throw line, walking unsteadily but attempting to conceal the effect of the collision. But he was far from right and he took all the time he could, bouncing the ball until the official warned him. Then he took the shot and the ball whizzed straight and true and

State was out in front of the national champions by a single point with twelve minutes left to play. Southwestern called time and looked unbelievingly at the scoreboard. The score: Southwestern 39, State 40.

In the State dressing room, Chip was lying on the rubbing table and the Southwestern doctor was examining his leg when Corrigan stuck his head in the door. "How is it, Murph?" he asked.

The doctor answered. "He's a lucky young man. Nothing broken. The ligament seems to be sprained. Probably be pretty stiff for a few days but he'll be all right."

"Then he can go home with us tonight?"

"Oh, sure. We'll have him walking before the game is over."

"What's the score, Coach?" Chip asked.

Corrigan grinned. "We're ahead. Jimmy sank your shot and just threw in another and Southwestern called time. I told Markley to line up and then ask for a time-out. We can gain a little extra time that way. The fellows are worried. They'll be glad to know you're all right."

"Not all right, Coach," the doctor said. "Far from it. But at least there's nothing broken. I'd advise you to get him to a doctor as soon as you get home."

"Murph will take care of that," Corrigan said. "Thanks a lot, Doc. Well, I've got to get back and hold that lead."

After Corrigan left, the doctor bandaged the knee and urged him to try it out by walking around the dressing room. "Exercise will help, Hilton. But stop when you feel tired. Well, I guess I can't do anything more for you. Sorry you got hurt. I'd like to have seen some more of you in action. How come you got away from Jeff Habley? I thought he knew every star in the country."

"My father went to State," Chip said simply. "Besides, all my friends go there and it's our state university. We're pretty proud of our school."

When the door closed, Kelly turned back to Chip. "Now you keep moving around, Chip, and I'll get back to the bench. Might be a good thing to get dressed before the game's over. Water won't hurt that bandage. I'll keep you posted on the score. Can't be more'n three or four minutes to the quarter."

Chip was in the shower when Kelly reappeared and one look at his long face told Chip the story. Kelly caught his glance and shook his head. "No good! Got us down by five, 46 to 41. Knee feel better? Good. I'll be back."

Chip was dressed the next time the trainer returned. "Bad," Kelly said disgustedly. "I've seen a lot of basketball, but I've never seen any team play as dirty as that bunch. I don't know how they get away with it."

"What's the score now, Murph?"

Kelly shook his head glumly. "Hate to tell you. Nineteen points—66 to 47. About five minutes left to play. Guess I'd better go back."

Chip packed his gear and sat down on the rubbing table. He could hear the roar of the crowd and then he heard the shot ending the game. Seconds later, the door opened and his teammates straggled in, thoroughly beaten and discouraged. And thoroughly aroused with anger. They were in no mood to talk about the game, but despite their anger and dejection, they didn't forget Chip. And the brief smiles of relief which crossed their lips when they learned the extent of his injury cut deeply into Chip's heart.

Yes, he sure was proud of his school and his teammates and his team. Fighting all the way and losing like gentlemen. . . .

The players dressed hurriedly and the taxicabs that whisked them away from the Southwestern field house couldn't do it fast enough. At that, they barely made the eleven-o'clock express. But it was a big relief to know that every turn of the wheels took them farther away from the evening's debacle —put distance between them and a sorry sports exhibition.

On Murph Kelly's orders, their Pullman had not been made up. And a lot of the gloom was dispelled by the sandwiches, milk, cookies, cokes, and ice cream Murph secured from the lounge car.

Food is a great morale builder for athletes. And as the miles put distance between State and the disastrous trouncing, their spirits lifted. Jimmy, Speed, Sky Bollinger, and Chip shared a double Pullman seat and Chip skillfully led the conversation around to the game.

"We were terrible," Sky said. "If I ever play bad basketball like that again I'll turn in my uniform. If it hadn't been for Jimmy, we wouldn't have scored fifty points."

"I never played football," Jimmy said grimly, "but if it's any worse than that kind of basketball . . . *excuse* me!"

"You took care of Ralk, all right," Speed said. "Tied him in knots."

"I wish someone would explain to me how Southwestern can get away with that kind of basketball," Jimmy said. "They surely can't play that way when they're on the road and in the tournaments."

"Rock scouted them when they were away from

LESSON IN SPORTSMANSHIP 95

home," Speed said shortly. "You know what he told us . . ."

"I guess it's a different league," Sky said thoughtfully. "They're big time and we're just another team."

"That's all right," Jimmy said, "but the rules ought to be the same for every team and all over the country. They play as if they wrote the rules."

"Anyone can beat the rules," Chip said softly. "Anyone who wants to play that kind of basketball."

"But how about the officials?" Jimmy persisted. "How come they let them get away with charging and pushing and tripping and busting you in the nose with their elbows and things like that?"

"Because they're Southwestern," Speed said. "They're the national champs. They can get away with murder."

"Not quite," Chip protested. "They just happen to be clever. It will catch up with them."

Speed smiled ruefully. "Better hurry up. Most of them are seniors and they'll be out of school."

"I wish *we* could catch up with them," Jimmy said. "I'd give five years of my life to see someone upset that dirty bunch." He tried to draw a deep breath. "You know something? I never told Murph, but I think I've got a cracked rib."

"Tell him now," Chip urged.

Jimmy shook his head and smiled. "I'll tell him in the morning. He's had a rough night."

"I'll say he has," Sky agreed. "He works like a dog and gives us the dickens and treats us like dirt, but he'd give you his right arm, and way down underneath he thinks anyone who plays for State is a king."

Speed nodded. "Right! Well, Sky, our berths are made up. Let's hit the sack. You take the upper."

"Why me?"

"So your long legs can stick out without tripping everyone who goes down the aisle. Good night, Chipper, Jimmy."

The porter was making up their berths and Jimmy continued the conversation. Jimmy was still disturbed by the humiliation and the dirty play. "It isn't fair," he said. "Remember when we were talking Sunday? About sportsmanship and your Golden Rule?"

"We'll have another chance, Jimmy. In the tournament, maybe."

"I'd give anything in the world to get even with that bunch."

Chip nodded. "I know. I feel the same way. They're fine players and don't have to play dirty to win. That's what I can't understand."

"Do you really think we'll have a chance in the tournament?"

"Every team has a chance. It would be nice to win it in your own home town, with your folks there to see you do it."

"My pop wouldn't walk across the street to see the President of the United States box the King of England."

"You mean he doesn't like athletics?"

"That's right. In fact, he doesn't know I'm playing. He'd hit the ceiling if he knew I wasn't spending all my time studying."

"Won't he find out when we play Wilson Tech?"

"I don't think so."

"But how about the papers?"

"He never reads American papers, particularly sports pages. You won't believe it, but we don't even have a telephone in the restaurant."

LESSON IN SPORTSMANSHIP 97

"No telephone? Why not?"

"A telephone would mean we were prosperous."

"What's wrong with that?"

"Nothing as far as I'm concerned, but that's the way it is. In China, the bandits kidnap a man if they think he is making money. Pop still thinks he is in the old country."

"You're kidding."

"I was never more serious. You ought to see our restaurant. It's decorated in red—that's a favorite Chinese color—with grotesque paintings of flowers and birds all over the place. And if a stray dog or cat wanders in, it becomes a member of the family just like that, because it's a sign of good luck. My sisters sneak them away, or there wouldn't be anything in the place but cats."

"Now you *are* kidding."

"No, I'm not. On my word of honor."

"Maybe you can change all that when you get through college," Chip suggested soberly.

Jimmy shrugged. "*If* I get through college," he repeated. "The way things are going at home, I'll be lucky to get through this semester."

"Business can't be that bad."

"Well," Jimmy admitted, "it might not be so bad if Pop could keep his help happy. But they're always walking out. I guess that's one of the biggest troubles with the restaurant. If he'd only listen to Tommy and me and dress up the place and serve American food as well as Chinese food, everything would be great. We've got a fine location."

Jimmy stopped suddenly and shook his head disgustedly. "There I go again, bothering you with my troubles."

"A friend's troubles are never a bother, Jimmy."

CHAPTER 11

SUBTLE AS A TECHNICAL FOUL

JIMMY LU CHUNG and Chip shared the sports headlines in the University papers the next day. The *News* said that Hilton had been the best player on the floor until he was injured and that Jimmy Lu Chung deserved those honors for the rest of the game. The *Herald* played up the fact that State held the lead early in the second half, and printed pictures of Chip and Jimmy.

The campus chatter was not so much concerned with State's defeat as with Southwestern's forty-first consecutive victory streak and the almost unbelievable home-floor consecutive win skein of 141 games.

Some mention was made of the extremely rough and reckless play and the poor officiating, but the students couldn't get the players to talk much about that part of the game. Coach Jim Corrigan and Henry Rockwell and their players didn't believe in alibis.

Chip's knee had stiffened up during the night and he walked several extra blocks on his way to report to Murph Kelly. Kelly was expecting him. "You walk pretty good," Kelly said in his usual gruff manner. "Any pain?"

SUBTLE AS A TECHNICAL FOUL 99

"None at all. Just feels tight and tired."

"Well, come on. Might as well get the bad news. Gave Doc the X-rays first thing this morning. Said to bring you right up."

There was no waiting and the nurse ushered Chip and Kelly directly into the examination room. Dr. Terring smiled a greeting and motioned Chip toward the table. "Let's have a look-see. Couldn't find anything wrong with it in the X-rays. Hmmm. . . . Not too bad. . . . Hurt when you walk?"

"No, sir."

"Murph's bandage helped, I guess. Yes, it's secure enough. Let him exercise lightly, Murph, but watch him. No massage, of course. Whirlpool will help."

"Want him to dress?"

"Not today. Perhaps Saturday."

"We've got a game on Saturday," Chip suggested.

Terring smiled. "We'll see . . ."

Kelly gave Chip a session in the whirlpool and a quick turn under the sun lamp. Then Chip sat up in the bleachers and watched practice. Corrigan was experimenting with a new line-up which included Markley, King, Di Santis, Thornhill, and Jimmy. But, as before, Jimmy couldn't blend into the set attack.

"He's a natural for a wide-open game," Chip breathed. "I wish Coach would give Speed and Sky and Bitsy and Jimmy and me a chance to use the fast break and a little more of a free attack."

Chip left early and walked slowly toward Main Street, trying to keep from limping. When he reached Main and Tenth, he continued on down to Pete's Place for a bite to eat before going to work. Pete was getting ready for the dinner rush and talked to Chip while he worked.

"Best cook or waiter I ever had, that Jimmy!"

"Is that so?" a cheery voice demanded. Jimmy entered just in time to hear Pete's words. "Well," he added, "I ought to be! Pop always had trouble with his cooks and I had to fill in. Want me to eat now, Pete?"

Pete nodded. "Sure, kid. Sit down there with Chip."

While Jimmy was eating Pete's roast beef special, he continued, "Cooks are aristocrats in the Chinese system, Chip. Servant system, that is—"

"I guess that's true all over the world. Especially the chefs."

"You couldn't tell my pop that. Labor means nothing to him. Everything's got to have material value. So he brings in a lot of cheap labor and pretty soon they learn the kind of wages cooks and waiters get at other places and they quit. Pop just can't seem to understand that the human element enters into everything—even cooking or waiting table. But the people he trains learn quickly enough. They find out what cooks and waiters get at other places and they quit."

"Everyone wants to make more money."

"Money isn't everything, Chip. The Chinese are different in that respect. Peace, comfort, and security are more important to them than actual wages. They want a little bonus each month to buy pork and wine, and that's about the limit of their concern about money. They're temperamental, too. If a popular headwaiter is fired, or you tell them they can't smoke or you don't let them off for the spring festival—they quit! Just like that!"

"That's different. Most of the workers I know are

SUBTLE AS A TECHNICAL FOUL 101

chiefly interested in the money they can make. The same goes for me! I'm late. See you after work."

Chip had a visitor about nine o'clock. Henry Rockwell sauntered into the stockroom and Chip greeted him warmly. There was a strong bond between Chip and the veteran mentor, and whenever Chip experienced some sort of difficulty, Rockwell invariably turned up.

"Thought I'd just check up on this knee business myself," Rockwell said. "Is it all right or not?"

"It's stiff and sore but there's no real pain, Coach. And I can use it fine, or at least pretty good."

I checked with Doc Terring and he said the same thing but I wanted to make sure. Do you think Ralk fouled you deliberately?"

"I don't know, Coach. I didn't see him. I took the shot and he must have dived over my shoulder to stop it. All I know is that he knocked me for a loop."

"What do you think of Southwestern's style of play?"

"I think the same as you," Chip replied wryly.

Rockwell shrugged. "By the way, what would you think of our chances in another game with them? With good officiating and everyone, including yourself—naturally, in good shape?"

"I don't know, Coach. They're good! They stopped our set attack cold."

"How about *our* defense?"

"They didn't have much trouble scoring on us. We're not big enough to stop them under the boards."

Rockwell nodded thoughtfully and paced back and forth across the room. "You're right, Chip. You can't play the other fellow's game and expect to win."

"I think the press attack you taught us in high school would give them a lot of trouble."

"Why?"

"They don't like to run or they don't appear to like it. Maybe it's because they haven't had to run. They use a strong collapsing defense and a deliberate power attack with a strong follow-in. I was thinking that if a team played them all over the court man to man and switched on every cross and took a lot of chances, they might get upset."

"But we don't have that kind of a team, Chip."

"Not the first five. But Jimmy Lu Chung would be terrific in an all-court press and Speed and Bitsy Reardon and Sky are fast and they can run all night . . ."

"And if Chip Hilton's knee was in good shape," Rockwell added, smiling, "you think it would be a pretty fair press team. Right? So do I! Tough part is the fact you're all sophomores. All except Lu Chung. And Coach Corrigan is dead set on his weave. But it's something to think about. I'm glad you're all right, but I want you to promise me you will quit the second your knee acts up. O.K.? Guess I'll be running along. See you tomorrow."

Chip reported to the gym early the next afternoon, and Corrigan and Henry Rockwell happened along while Kelly was working on the knee.

"He's coming along fine, Coach," Kelly said. "Gonna let him work out this afternoon, or at least do a little shooting."

"I'm glad to hear that," Corrigan said. "How about the game tomorrow night?"

"He's coming in tomorrow morning and again in the afternoon, and Doc said he'd know by that time. He said he'd be ready for the Wilson Tech game."

SUBTLE AS A TECHNICAL FOUL 103

Corrigan and Rockwell walked slowly up the steps to the office. Settling themselves comfortably in their chairs, they talked about Chip and the team in general. Corrigan was depressed and Rockwell tried to cheer him up.

"Three and one," Corrigan said gloomily. "What a record! What's wrong with the team, Rock?"

"It's a pretty tough schedule."

"Tough for other teams, too. I thought we were going to have a great year. We certainly have plenty of talent."

"It's early," Rockwell said cheerfully. "Did you ever think about using two teams? One year I had a bunch of veterans and some youngsters almost as wild as the Southwestern fans. They were a whole lot like Reardon, Morris, Lu Chung, and Bollinger. . . .

"Well, I used them as a sort of change-of-pace outfit; played the veterans for part of the game and then stuck in the kids. It was something to see. Fans loved it. It might be the answer to your problem."

Corrigan frowned thoughtfully and studied the veteran coach with knowing eyes. "I suppose you would play Hilton with that bunch—"

Rockwell nodded gravely, "Oh, sure."

"Oh, sure!" Corrigan mimicked. "You know something, Rock," he continued thoughtfully, "you're about as subtle as a technical foul." He banged his fist down on the desk. "All right, I'll give it a try. Tomorrow night!"

Doc Terring and Murph Kelly were waiting when Chip reported at nine o'clock Saturday morning. After the bandage was removed, Doc Terring checked the knee carefully. Then he replaced the bandage and went up on the gym floor and had

Chip run around the court several times. Then Doc Terring checked the knee carefully again. "All right, Murph," he said at last, "give him a little whirlpool this morning and the lamp this afternoon."

"What about the game?"

"I'll talk to you about that later."

Following the lamp treatment and another examination by Doc Terring that afternoon, Chip felt so good he wanted to sprint all the way to State Drug, convinced he would be ready to play that night. But Murph Kelly and Coach Jim Corrigan had other ideas.

In the dressing room, Murph Kelly checked the bandage and told him he could dress. Chip suited up and waited hopefully during Corrigan's pregame talk.

"This one is a must! So we're going to try something new. We're going to match man to man when we line up, but when they cross on the offense, we're going to switch. And we'll take a few chances and try to make some interceptions.

"On the offense, we'll fast-break when we get the chance, and if we can't get a three-on-two or a two-on-one situation, we'll go into the weave. All right, we'll start with Markley, Thornhill, King, Di Santis, and Lu Chung."

In the pregame warm-up drill, Chip loosened up gradually, favoring his leg but moving without pain. But he wasn't right and he knew it. And so did Murph Kelly and Coach Corrigan. They were watching him closely.

"What do you think, Murph? What did Doc Terring say?"

"Said to use him if you had to, but only for a few minutes at a time. Better let him sit for a while."

SUBTLE AS A TECHNICAL FOUL

"Hope I don't need him. But we've got to win this one or we're sunk."

So Chip sat the bench and suffered with the fans as Northern State slowly but surely drew away from the desperate Statesmen. Jimmy was magnificent on the defense, stealing the ball and dribbling the length of the court for several quick scores. And when State managed to work a fast break, he was the spearhead of the attack. But he was throttled when State went into the weave; his lightning ability to take advantage of openings was too fast for the veterans and time after time they failed to hit him with the ball.

With the score 40 to 25 in favor of the visitors and five minutes left to play in the first half, Corrigan put Chip in for Di Santis. State took on new life right away. Chip hit with three sets and a free throw, and the teams left the court with the score: Northern State 41, State 32.

State looked better the second half. Corrigan used the same line-up which started the game and the teams battled on even terms. But even terms couldn't make up the deficit and at the start of the fourth quarter, Northern State led: 55 to 44.

When the players gathered in front of the bench, Corrigan almost shocked them out of their suits. "All right," he said decisively. "We're going to use the press. I want you to forget all about the weave and the slow advance and chase them all over the court. Let's go!"

Chip and the other bench warmers who had surrounded the starters dropped back down on the bench. Chip nudged Speed and glanced significantly at Bitsy Reardon. Bitsy nodded. This was the kind of basketball they liked. . . .

Out on the floor, the veterans were attempting the press. But it backfired. They had been drilled too long in Corrigan's slow advance and deliberate weave; switched at the wrong time; failed to cover up on a try for an interception, and, with the exception of Jimmy, completely botched up the game. Northern State gleefully took advantage of their misplays, and when Corrigan yelled for time, the visitors led, 68 to 51, with eight minutes left to play.

"All right, Hilton! Reardon! Bollinger! Morris! Report for Markley, Thornhill, Di Santis, and King. Lu Chung stays in!"

Chip and his sophomore pals raced to the scoring table and back to surround Corrigan and Lu Chung. "Now listen!" Corrigan rasped excitedly. "Same thing! Press 'em all over the court. Take chances! Eight minutes and seventeen points behind. Nothing to lose! Go get 'em!"

They got 'em! Speed and Jimmy and Bitsy were lightning fast in their reflexes; interceptive minded, superior judges of distance and timing, and they swarmed all over Northern State's small men. Sky and Chip paired up against the two big men and froze them clear out of the play.

The State fans could scarcely follow the lightning-fast action on the floor, but they could see the scoreboard, and as the numbers behind the home-team position flickered again and again they realized that something tremendous was happening to their team and they wanted to be a part of it. They rose to their feet en masse and yelled and screamed and stamped until it seemed that the building would come tumbling down.

"Fight team. Fight! Yea, State! Yea, Lu Chung!"

"Lu Chung! Lu Chung! Lu Chung!"

SUBTLE AS A TECHNICAL FOUL 107

Jimmy was all over the floor, making interceptions, double-teaming opponents, dribbling furiously for the State goal, and drawing two and sometimes three of the opponents to him in a vain attempt to stop his mad progress toward the basket. Then Jimmy would slip the ball to Speed or Bitsy for an easy lay-up or, more often, fire the ball back to Chip for a clear set shot.

Chip was content to remain in the backcourt, take it easy, and wait for Jimmy, Speed, or Bitsy to get the ball. Sky was back with him and did most of the running, covering up so that Chip could protect his knee.

Chip took his set shots when none of his teammates were uncovered, and without bearing down on his knee, got twelve of the twenty-six points State scored in those mad eight minutes. Northern State battled furiously but couldn't hold the lead. Chip tied the score at 75 to 75, with thirty seconds left to play, and Jimmy wrapped it up with an interception and a two-pointer a split second before the buzzer.

The game ended with the fans, the veterans on the bench, the coaches, and the visiting players completely exhausted. The final score: State 77, Northern State 75.

CHAPTER 12

WE HAVEN'T GOT THE HORSES

STATE'S CO-CAPTAINS were the first to reach Jimmy after the final buzzer. Kirk and Randy ushered him off the court, patting him on the back and ruffling his hair all the way to the dressing room. The fans gave Jimmy a standing ovation until he passed from sight. Jimmy had arrived at the door of stardom; had thrilled every State partisan by his dazzling performance in the action-packed last-minute victory surge, and had won almost single-handed a game most fans had given up as lost.

Chip and Speed and Bitsy and Sky came in for their share of the glory when the team reached the dressing room, and upstairs in the athletic office, Jim Corrigan dropped wearily down in his desk chair and breathed a deep sigh of relief.

Rockwell settled himself comfortably in his favorite chair and grinned appreciatively at the happy coach. "That was one for the books," he said. "Nice comeback."

"Thanks to your idea," Corrigan said thankfully. "It was your idea and it worked. I've been using the kids all wrong. They put on the press as if they had played that way all their lives. Lu Chung was sensational."

"Chip wasn't bad," Rockwell added dryly. "By the way, he suggested the press and the sophomore combination with Lu Chung to me the other day and I passed it on to you. I'm glad I did."

"Chip's not only a great player; he uses his head," Corrigan said. "And what an eye! I never saw anyone shoot like he can. What a combination he and Lu Chung make."

"You had me wondering a bit when you put on the press with Markley and Thornhill and the other starters."

"I had to do that, Rock. Had to give the veterans a chance at it so they would find out they couldn't handle it. Worked out all right, but it was too close for comfort."

"Going to stick with it?"

"And how! I'm going to use your suggestion . . . two teams. But I think it will be good strategy to keep the press team under cover and use it only when we can't win with straight basketball. Sound O.K. to you?"

"It sure does. In fact, that's the way I've always used the press. Had a special team which could handle it and worked them on every phase of it every day. Then, when I wanted to surprise a team or when we couldn't win with our regular style, I'd send in the press team."

Corrigan shot forward in his chair. "Say," he said excitedly, "that gives me an idea! We won't get far playing straight against the tough teams in the tournament. We haven't got the horses. But if we worked the kids on the press every day we might even surprise Southwestern. . . .

"Boy, that's one team every coach in the country would like to see lose. Especially me! I'll never get over the treatment they gave us last week. You think the press would work against them?"

"It's worth trying. Chip thinks it will work." Rockwell hesitated and stroked his chin reflectively. "Er —as a suggestion, Jim, why don't you concentrate on the kids and try to get along without the press until the tournament. I believe you can beat Wilson Tech and Cathedral without the press. Then, if you can get by in the tournament with straight basketball until you run into Southwestern—*if* you run into them—maybe you can engineer the greatest upset of all times."

"Be just our luck to draw them in the first round."

"All the better," Rockwell said crisply. "Then you *would* surprise them. Well, I guess I'll go home." He paused at the door. "Tonight you can sleep, right? Stop worrying, Jim. You've got a good team."

Chip and Jimmy managed to get away from their happy teammates and started for work. Chip was tired and tempted to go home, but State Drug was exceptionally busy on game nights. So he trudged along with Jimmy, thankful that the training curfew was not in effect.

Then they got a break. Despite the hails of several groups, a taxi sped up beside them and the door opened before the cab screeched to a stop. "Want a ride, Hilton? We're going right past State Drug."

Chip peered in at the speaker and recognized Sky Bollinger's father. "Got room for both of us?"

Mr. Bollinger pulled down the folding seats. "Sure. Plenty of room. Wanted to talk to you, anyway. Some game you boys put up tonight. Move over, Bobby.

Chip, you know Mrs. Bollinger and Bobby, I guess." He extended his hand to Jimmy. "My name is Bollinger. I'm Sky Bollinger's father. This is Mrs. Bollinger. Shake hands with Bobby. Sure glad to meet you, Lu Chung. Never saw anyone put on a passing exhibition in my life as you put on tonight. Some shooting, Chip. Sky's coming along. Right, Chip? Thanks to you." He leaned forward and tapped Jimmy on the shoulder. "Guess you didn't know Chip here helped me straighten out my whole family last year, did you?"

"Now, father . . ." Mrs. Bollinger protested.

"Well, it's true, isn't it? Made Bobby here shooting champion of the country in his class and made a man of Sky. Straightened him out until he's a pretty fair country ballplayer now. Hope Corrigan keeps you fellows together as a team. Played myself a few years back and I know a real team when I see it . . ."

Mrs. Bollinger laughed. "A few years . . ."

Chip and Jimmy listened to Mr. Bollinger all the way down to State Drug. And when they got out of the taxi they accepted an invitation to dinner at the Bollinger home the next afternoon.

"Wow!" Jimmy said. "No wonder Sky can run. He'd have to be fast to escape that—"

"He's a nice man," Chip said, laughing. "But he's hoop crazy. We'll have a good time at their house. They're real nice people. See you after work."

Jimmy impulsively grasped Chip by the arm. "Take care of that leg, Chip," he said solicitously. "We haven't got much of a team without you." He hesitated a moment and then continued, "Another thing. I couldn't help hearing all the nice things Mr. Bollinger was saying in the taxi and I just want you to know he expressed my sentiments, too, except that he's better qualified to put it into words. I guess you know what I mean. See you later."

Soapy and Fireball Finley and Philip Whittemore were struggling to keep up with the fountain demands of their noisy customers, but they spotted Chip as soon as he came through the door. "Hey, Chip! Attaboy! Big win!"

The greeting was taken up by the customers and Chip had a difficult time getting through the crowd. He breathed a sigh of relief when he gained the stockroom but he caught it again from his assistant, fifteen-year-old Eddie Redding. While Eddie was shooting questions at him about the game, Chip hustled into a white fountain coat. His job was in the stockroom but he always helped his pals at the fountain when there was a big rush.

Meanwhile, business was booming at Pete's Place. This after-game rush was all new to Pete. A few of the college students who appreciated good food at inexpensive prices had always favored Pete's Place, but with the addition of Jimmy to the staff, the campus business had increased by leaps and bounds.

Tonight, Pete couldn't keep up with the rush. But he loved it! The customer discussions were all concerned with the game and Jimmy was the center of attention. But Jimmy didn't stop in his work to gab; he worked as he played basketball, his hands and his feet flying, doing the work of three waiters. Pete kept going too, but he listened avidly to the conversations.

"Nice going, Jimmy! What's the coach been saving you for—the prom?"

"What you and Hilton got—a partnership? He takes the shots and all you gotta do is get the ball. Some system."

WE HAVEN'T THE HORSES 113

Jimmy grinned happily. "If you could shoot like Hilton, I'd get the ball for you, too!"

"Aw, I couldn't make baskets from the bleachers!"

"Chip Hilton could!" Jimmy retorted.

The old-line customers who sat on the stools in front of the counter had listened to the student chatter and now one of them ventured into the conversation. "You fellows won't last long in that tournament up in Clinton. That's my home town and I've seen some of the teams they get in the Invitational. They get the best."

"Clinton's my home town, too," Jimmy said. "I've seen a lot of those tournaments. We're going to win this one."

"You guys better take Wilson Tech and Cathedral first," one of the students bantered.

"We'll take 'em!" Jimmy said. "We'll take 'em all if Chip's knee holds up."

"He didn't move very much tonight."

"You *have* to move on that big court in Wilson Tech's new field house," the man who had spoken previously observed. "It's more like a football field than a basketall court."

"We can move."

"How about Hilton? How about his knee?"

Jimmy was ready for that question. "He'll run when the time comes," he said confidently.

"That's the court they use for the tournament, isn't it?"

"Sure is! Tech's in the tournament, too."

"Seems to me they get all the breaks. People who know tell me a home court means a ten- to fifteen-point advantage for the home team."

"The team is the thing!" Jimmy said. "Not the court!"

"Tech is one of the best in the country."

"Yes, and they'll be laying for you, Jimmy. They'll be out to show up the home-town boy."

Jimmy nodded grimly. "I know. I've been waiting for a chance at them, too. Ever since I was in high school."

Later, when Chip and Soapy came in for a snack before going home, Pete's Place was still filled. Pete and Jimmy were working side by side behind the counter, keeping up a constant chatter with the hungry customers. Pete's face was covered with perspiration but Jimmy looked cool and composed.

"Either of you gentlemen lookin' for a job?" Pete asked, mopping his forehead and winking at Jimmy. "Business is so good, Jimmy and I are thinkin' about goin' to Florida for the rest of the winter."

"How about selling the place?" Soapy asked. "I've got a coupla hundred bucks I'm not using."

"Talk to my partner," Pete said, jerking a thumb in Jimmy's direction. "It's up to him. S'pose you go along with these two gentlemen, Jimmy, and discuss the terms."

It was good fun, but while the three pals were walking leisurely home, the talk swung to basketball and struck a serious note. "Southwestern won again," Jimmy said abruptly. "Number forty-two. Heard it on Gray's program. Hundred and forty-two in a row at home."

"No one seems able to stop them," Chip said.

"You'll stop 'em!" Soapy said stoutly. "In the tournament! Wait and see if I'm not right."

They continued on, thinking about Southwestern and the tournament. When they reached the corner where Jimmy turned to go home, they stopped for a second. "The two big ambitions in my life right

WE HAVEN'T THE HORSES 115

now," Jimmy said, "are first to beat Wilson Tech Wednesday night in Clinton and then whip Southwestern in the tournament."

"Then you fellows better get some sleep," Soapy said.

"Going to church with us in the morning, Jimmy?"

"I'd like to, Chip."

"O.K. We'll meet you right here at ten o'clock."

After the church services the next morning, Soapy left for Mitzi Savrill's home and Chip and Jimmy walked all the way across University to the Bollingers. As Chip has promised, Jimmy had a wonderful time. Mr. Bollinger seemed content to listen to the basketball talk and the plans for the tournament. Mrs. Bollinger was the star of the show, proving to be a charming hostess and serving a dinner which drew enthusiastic comments from guests and family.

"That's the kind of food my pop ought to serve," Jimmy said. "I'm glad we don't have a game tonight. I don't think I can walk home."

Jimmy was still lauding Mrs. Bollinger's cooking when Chip left him later that afternoon. "My," Jimmy said, grinning and patting his stomach happily, "that beats Pete's Place a mile. See you tomorrow morning in the library."

But Chip didn't see Jimmy the next morning. Jimmy wasn't at the library nor with the gang at the Student Union. So Chip walked briskly across the campus and down Main Street. He passed the drugstore and turned down Tenth to Pete's Place. Pete was leaning on the cash register, staring moodily out the window.

"Have you seen Jimmy?" Chip asked.

Pete nodded slowly. "Yeah, I saw him," he said

glumly. "Came in here first thing this morning looking like he'd lost his best friend. Said he had to quit, had to go home."

"Quit? You mean quit the job?"

"That's right. He wanted his money and I gave it to him."

"But what about school?"

"Quit school too! Said he was shippin' his trunk home and for me to tell everybody good-by. It's got me down. I don't care whether I keep the joint open or not . . . couldn't have thought more of Jimmy if he was my own son."

CHAPTER 13

THE NEW CHINA TEA HOUSE

TIMETABLE travel time between University and Clinton is listed as slightly under six hours. But it seemed like sixty hours to Jimmy Lu Chung. Ordinarily, he would have enjoyed the ride; read a little, sauntered forward to the Pullman car for a leisurely lunch, and probably entered into a casual conversation with a fellow traveler. But not this trip.

Jimmy sat alone in a seat by the window, gazing with sad, uninterested eyes at fields and farmhouses and small towns and roads and fences and trees and the never-ending line of telephone poles that whizzed past in a steady blur. He tried to tell himself that the yellow piece of paper in his pocket was a figment of his imagination; that the words pasted on the paper advising him that his father was seriously ill, and that he must give up school, was part of a bad dream. Maybe there wasn't any telegram and maybe he wasn't even on this train.

But it was no use and he remembered how he had envisioned this train ride to Clinton with the team, to play against Wilson Tech, and suddenly the lump in his chest and his throat swelled up and he felt that he couldn't bear the pain. And just about then, back in University, Chip was standing beside the cashier's desk reading the letter Jimmy had written and mailed to him at the drugstore.

Sunday night

Dear Chip:

By the time this letter reaches you I will be on my way home. My father is sick and it is necessary for me to go home and take care of the restaurant. I guess a lot of Pop's sickness is due to money matters and worry over the restaurant and my place is with him and the family.

Will you please explain to Coach Corrigan why I had to leave and say good-by to all the fellows and Coach Rockwell. I guess I will have to forget about college and basketball, but I'll never forget all the things you did for me.

Always your friend,
Jimmy

Chip didn't feel much like going to practice that afternoon. But he had to give Jimmy's message to Coach Corrigan, so he got an early start and walked slowly back to the campus and up to the athletic office. Coach Corrigan and Henry Rockwell were bending over some papers on the desk.

Corrigan looked up and motioned for Chip to come in. "Hiya, Chip," he said cheerfully. "You're early! Come on in. We're just looking over the Wilson Tech scouting notes. Anything on your mind?"

"Quite a lot," Chip said quietly. "I'm afraid I've got some bad news." He handed Jimmy's letter to Coach Corrigan saying: "Jimmy has to quit school."

"Quit school?" Corrigan echoed. "Oh, no!" He dropped down in his chair and read the letter without speaking. When he finished, he handed the

NEW CHINA TEA HOUSE 119

paper to Rockwell. "What next?" he said bitterly.

Rockwell finished the letter and returned it to Chip. "Can't we get him back? Can't his father hire someone to run the place? Hasn't he got any brothers?"

"He has one brother, Coach, but he doesn't live at home."

"Can't they send for him? Wouldn't that make more sense than pulling Jimmy out of school and ruining a fine science career? I don't get it. I think we ought to call his father, Jim."

"Do you know Jimmy's telephone number in Clinton, Chip?" Corrigan asked.

"He doesn't have a telephone at his home, Coach."

"How about the restaurant?"

Chip tried to explain about the telephone and the eldest son and the rest of Jimmy's family difficulties, but Corrigan and Rockwell couldn't understand that sort of thing. They sat there, looking at each other and then at Chip, and back again, everything about them expressing disappointment.

"Well," Corrigan said at last, "we'll leave it in your hands. Just as soon as we get to Clinton, you check up with Jimmy and let us know how soon he can get back in school. Tell him we're counting on him playing against Wilson Tech, too."

"Jimmy is vital to our plans right now, Chip," Rockwell added. "In fact, he's the key to our whole tournament campaign. Present company excepted."

News of Jimmy's difficulties quickly spread through the squad and Corrigan might as well have called off practice for all the scrimmage benefited the players. Jimmy's popularity had soared after his fine play against Northern State, and his loss was a blow to everyone. After a short session under the

120   TOURNAMENT CRISIS

lamp, Chip went to work. It was a long evening.

Murph Kelly let Chip take part in a few of the drills the next afternoon and then put him under the lamp. And that night when he dropped in to see Pete on his way home, his knee felt as good as new. Pete handed him a letter.

"Give this to Jimmy, Chip. And try to get him back, will you? If it's a matter of money, I can help. Don't have much, coupla thousand, maybe, but he can have it."

"I think it's more a matter of family problems than money, Pete. Anyway, I'll know the whole story when I get back here Thursday."

Chip was asleep when Soapy came in from work and the redhead didn't even turn on the light. And in the morning, Soapy insisted on accompanying Chip to the train. At the depot he kidded everyone in sight and got Chip a Clinton paper and barely got off the train before the porter closed the door. "Give my best to Jimmy, Chip!" he yelled. "And if there's any way I can help . . ."

Chip opened the Clinton paper to the sports section. The first thing which met his eyes was a streamer across the top of the page.

NATIONAL CHAMPIONS IN DOUBLE-HEADER HERE TONIGHT

Southwestern Meets Wesleyan—Tech Plays State

Local basketball fans will have a preview of the Holiday Invitational Tournament tonight at WT field house when three of the competing teams, including the defending champion, Southwestern, meet in a double bill. Southwestern is expected to register its forty-third consecutive victory without too much difficulty since Wesleyan is comparatively weak.

NEW CHINA TEA HOUSE

In the nightcap, Tech may find a tartar in State which is coming along fast after a slow start.

The page was studded with pictures of Southwestern's great players surrounding their All-America teammates, Tom Bordon and Ralph Ralk. Chip turned to the next page and found the Wilson Tech squad featured in a group picture. Directly below was a photo of himself.

CHIP HILTON

State Sophomore Sensation to Face Tech Tonight

Tech Out to Stop High Scoring Marksman

Wilson Tech is facing two tasks tonight at the WT field house: the protection of their current season victory skein, and holding Chip Hilton, State's high-scoring sophomore marksman, in check.

Hilton has played in four games and has scored 93 markers in 69 minutes for an average of 1⅜ points per minute. The All-America quarterback is showing the way on the hardcourt just as he did last fall on the gridiron. Reporting late because of football, the blond bomber immediately broke into the starting line-up. He suffered a knee injury at Southwestern (25 points in 24 minutes) a week ago, but is reported to be in good shape for the game tonight.

"I hope, I hope," Chip murmured, closing the paper. He rested until lunch and afterward slept until the train arrived in Clinton. Right after the team had registered at the hotel he reported to Rockwell and took a taxi to the New China Tea House.

"Practice is at four o'clock at the Tech field house!" Rockwell warned him. "Be on time. Bring Jimmy with you."

The taxi driver knew exactly where to go and it took less than ten minutes to reach Chip's destination. The New China Tea House was attractively fronted with bamboo and Chinese characters. Chip gave it a quick glance and hurried inside, eager to see his friend. Inside the dining room he paused uncertainly; there wasn't a soul in sight. He hesitated and looked around. The interior was exactly as Jimmy had described it. The walls were covered with painted flowers and birds in garish colors, and dusty, old-fashioned lighting fixtures hung from the ceiling.

Just as Chip was going to call out, a waiter came slowly forward and bowed. "Is Jimmy here?" Chip asked. "Jimmy Lu Chung?"

The waiter bowed and nodded. "Please to be seated." He led the way to a small table and waited until Chip had seated himself. Then he bowed and walked quietly away. He had scarcely passed from Chip's view when the curtain at the back of the room parted and Jimmy came hurrying forward.

"Welcome, Chip. I knew you would come. How about something to eat?"

"Can't, Jimmy. We eat at five o'clock. How is your father?"

The happy expression vanished from Jimmy's face. "Not well, Chip. Everything has gone wrong. Pop has been sick for nearly a month and didn't tell me, and then he had trouble with the cooks and waiters and most of them left. Besides, business has been terrible. Everything looks pretty hopeless."

Chip gave him Pete's letter. "He misses you, Jimmy. We all miss you. Coach Corrigan and Coach Rockwell want you to come right back to school. Isn't

NEW CHINA TEA HOUSE 123

there something we can do? Pete said he could help if money would do any good."

"Money would help but it would be just postponing the inevitable," Jimmy said despondently. "There's a lot more to it than money."

"Couldn't you play just tonight?"

"Not a chance, Chip. I've got to forget basketball and school and everything else except my responsibilities as the eldest son."

"I wish I could do something. Maybe I could talk to your father."

"It would be time thrown away. He detests sports. No, my place is here."

"Your place is in college. Anyway, you can come to the game, can't you? I've got some tickets."

"I can't even do that, Chip. I've got to stay on the job. Not that there's much business."

"I can't see why your brother doesn't run the restaurant. Especially since he likes the restaurant business."

"Tommy could do a wonderful job if Pop would only change his methods. But Tommy will never co-operate as long as we try to sell Chinese food in a spot where there's no demand for it. That was the cause of the trouble between Tommy and Pop. The reason Tommy left home."

"But doesn't he have responsibilities, too? The same as you?"

"He has responsibilities, but the eldest son, the first son, is dedicated to carrying on the family name and assuming the leadership in family problems. No, it's up to me and there's no way out."

They sat a long while in silence as friends often do while seeking the solution to a difficult problem. Chip had been slowed down but he wasn't quitting.

"There's got to be a way," he said stubbornly. "Just got to be! Let's talk it over later. Think you could get off to come to the train? We don't leave until twelve forty."

Jimmy laughed shortly. "I'll be there. This place is deserted after eleven o'clock. Come on outside and I'll show you how to get to the field house." Jimmy stood in the entrance until Chip had passed from sight. Then he turned dejectedly and walked back through the door of the New China Tea House.

Chip was early. Southwestern had just finished shooting practice and the players were lounging in the bleachers. He glanced at them and sat down to wait for his teammates. While he waited, he thought about Jimmy's problem.

When the State squad arrived, Chip told Rockwell what had transpired at the New China Tea House and then joined the team. He dressed quickly, anxious to get the feel of the court and try his shots. But he didn't have much chance to practice. Several photographers appeared from nowhere, seemingly, and insisted that he pose for a number of pictures. In the background he could hear the ridicule of the Southwestern players.

"Shotsky in person!"

"The heaver fires again!"

"Yeah, Chip shots by Hilton!"

"A one-man team, that's all!"

Chip was burning but he ignored the gibes and concentrated on his shots. But every word of ridicule strengthened his resolve to play the game of his life against Wilson Tech and fired him with an intense desire for another chance at Southwestern.

"If we could only meet them in the tournament . . ." he whispered to himself.

NEW CHINA TEA HOUSE 125

It was hard to take the taunts without fighting back. But Chip concealed the bitterness in his heart and kept his head. And it was this control of his emotions which gained him a friend. As he left the floor, a youngster about his own height and age stopped him. "Hello, Hilton. My name is Moran. Greg Moran. I'm captain of the Tech team. I've been sitting here listening to those Southwestern fellows and I just had to introduce myself and tell you how much I admire your self-control. I don't think I could have taken it."

"They were just kidding."

"Kidding or not, it wasn't good sportsmanship. Not that you could expect those fellows to be good sports. I know all about that crowd."

Before Moran left, he and Chip had become good friends. And when Southwestern ran out on the court to warm up for their game with Wesleyan later that night, Chip and Greg were sitting side by side in the player section like old friends.

During the first half of the game, Chip learned that his new friend was a senior and was majoring in engineering. Greg knew Jimmy Lu Chung and all about the New China Tea House. "Jimmy and I were in the same class in high school and played basketball together. He's a fine fellow."

"He sure is!"

"Be *something* if he and I lined up against each other tonight."

"Not much chance. He had to drop out of school."

"Oh, no! Why?"

"His father is sick and he has to take charge of the restaurant." Chip told Greg all about Jimmy's trouble and how badly the team needed him. "His father is dead set against sports, I guess."

Greg nodded understandingly. "*Now* I remember. Jimmy had a tough time playing when he was in high school. Come to think of it, I believe that was the reason he didn't go to Tech. Guess he figured he could play basketball at State but Tech would be too close to home."

The first half ended, then, with Southwestern leading Wesleyan by a score of 42 to 19 and they parted to suit up, each wishing the other good luck. Chip couldn't help but compare this kind of hospitality with the reception he and his teammates had received at Southwestern.

And when Chip and his teammates came out on the floor for their pregame warm-up, Chip found it was a different sports crowd, too. The cheerleaders led the home fans in a rousing cheer for State and the Tech band played the State Alma Mater. The score of the first game was still registered on the board and Chip saw that the champions had won their forty-third straight game with ease. The score: Southwestern 92, Wesleyan 44.

It looked like Wilson Tech was going to have an easy time, too. It was a solid ball club and used a sharp, short-passing attack which permitted few mistakes. On the defense, they played straight man to man. Chip got nine points in the first quarter and eleven in the second. But despite his twenty points, State left the court at the half with Tech ahead by a score of 47 to 38.

The Southwestern players had been seated in the first row of seats along the side of the court and began to leave to catch their train just as Chip and the rest of the State players left the floor.

"You fellows going to drop out of the tournament?"

"You fellows going to drop out of the tournament?" Ralk needled insolently

Ralk needled insolently. "It's for college teams! Or didn't you know?"

"We know," Markley rejoined coolly. "And we'll be there."

"For the first game, maybe," Bordon chimed in. "Why don't you guys try volleyball?"

"That's an idea," Randy Thornhill agreed calmly. "We might meet a team that knew something about sportsmanship, a few gentlemen."

"You wouldn't know how to act," Ralk retorted. "Hey, Hilton! Hey, Blond Bomber! Keep shootin'! You're bound to make a few if you keep heavin'!"

Chip said nothing, but once again he was fired with a grim determination to even the score with Southwestern. "If we only had Jimmy," he murmured fiercely. "We've *got* to get him back!"

CHAPTER 14

A NEW FIELD HOUSE RECORD

GREG MORAN was a fine basketball player, a good captain, and a gentleman. He possessed a fine shooting eye, and was having one of the best nights of his career. Greg was the leading scorer of his team and was averaging about twenty-five points per game. At the half he had twenty-two points and the fans were aware that he had a good chance to break the WT field house scoring record of fifty-three points. In the second half Greg took up where he had left off in the first and scored five straight points, putting Tech fourteen points out in front. Kirk Markley called a time-out and the State players ringed around Corrigan in front of the State bench.

"I've got four personals, Coach," Markley said. "I can't stop Moran without fouling."

"All right," Corrigan said briskly. "Switch with Chip. Chip, you take Moran. You've got to stop him."

"Chip will stop him," Speed muttered.

Moran smiled when Chip lined up against him after the time-out. "I've got company, huh?" he said, extending his hand.

Chip smiled in return and then sobered. This was for keeps and State needed this game. He was aware that Greg had scored a lot of points but had not given any thought to the shots his new friend used. He found out quick enough. While Chip was thinking about it, Greg passed off, faked a hard cut, dropped back, and took a return pass. Then, just as Chip would have done, he fired a set shot over Chip's head which never touched the rim.

"Sorry, old boy," Greg said, falling back on the defense.

"You won't get me with that one again," Chip said ruefully.

State was playing well, but Tech held the fourteen-point lead right up to the end of the third quarter. Chip garnered twelve points to bring his total to thirty-two, while Moran had scored another basket and a foul to bring his total to thirty points. The fans were cheering both players, now, keenly aware that Greg and Chip both might break the record.

During the time-out, Corrigan studied the scoreboard. "Seventy-one to fifty-seven," he said worriedly. "Ten minutes left to play and fourteen points behind. What do you think, fellows?"

"Better press," Markley said worriedly. "Try Morris and Reardon and Bollinger for Randy and Butcher and me. *We're* not getting anywhere."

"O.K.," Corrigan said briskly. "We've got nothing to lose."

State lined up with Sky Bollinger at center, Biz Gowdy and Speed Morris at the forwards, Bitsy Reardon and Chip at the guard positions. It was a small team but it was speedy. Gowdy was the only member of the group who was not exceptionally fast. And it was this tremendous team speed which caused Tech's downfall. Before they could

FIELD HOUSE RECORD 131

adjust themselves to the change of pace in State's attack, Chip had scored four quick jumpers and had slipped Speed the ball for two easy lay-ups. That brought the score up to 71 to 69, and Greg Moran called for a Tech time-out.

"We've got 'em going," Corrigan said breathlessly, glancing at the clock. "Seven minutes to play! Keep it up! Give the ball to Chip. He's hot!"

Corrigan didn't have to stress that; the fans had switched from Moran to Chip now, because Greg had fallen behind in the scoring. Chip had forty points while Greg had only thirty-three.

But the fans knew also there was enough time left for State to win the game. And the scoring record was secondary compared to the loss of the game.

State made a lot of mistakes during the next six minutes, but Tech made more. With the score 88 to 87 in Tech's favor, Moran called another time-out. Chip had tied the individual scoring record on the last play and now had fifty-three points.

Chip heard the mixed cheering of the fans; the encouraging shouts for the home team and the entreaties for a new record. But he wasn't interested in records. He wanted his *team* to win the game. This was for the team and State.

Bitsy pressed and dove for the ball. But he missed, and Speed and Chip were forced to drop back into their own backcourt to cover for him. The Tech guards brought the ball swiftly up the court, watching the clock to escape the ten-second penalty and yet use every possible second before starting a freeze. Chip watched the clock, too. Fifty-five seconds . . . fifty. . . . Then the Tech guards were across the ten-second line and into their front court and Bitsy had caught up with his opponent.

Chip was playing dummy and so was Speed. Bitsy began to chase the ball. His mad dives and threats had the Tech players on edge and they forgot about Speed and Chip. Then it happened! Speed leaped forward; intercepted the ball with ten seconds left to play. Chip saw it coming and broke for the State basket. He took Speed's toss out in front all alone and dribbled upcourt at full speed, concentrating on the basket. Behind him, he could hear Greg Moran pounding the court, practically breathing down his neck. Then, above the exhortations and shouts of the fans, Chip heard Sky Bollinger shout: "Shoot, Chip! Shoot!"

But Chip didn't shoot. Just as Greg leaped into the air to stop the lay-up, Chip bounced the ball to Sky on the other side of the basket. Sky was so surprised that he nearly missed the bounce pass. But he caught it and leaped high in the air. And—missed the shot!

The ball hit the backboard, rebounded, rolled around the iron rim and started to fall into the lane. Chip recovered his balance just under the basket, leaped with all his power, and stabbed at the ball. His fingers barely touched the leather but he flicked the ball back up on the rim. There, the ball balanced for a second and then fell through the hoop just as the buzzer sounded. State had won 89 to 88, and Chip had set a new WT field house record of fifty-five points.

A casual spectator would have thought State had won the national championship. The players ganged up on Chip, pounding his back and shoulders and pumping his hand for all they were worth. The Tech players weren't far behind and the first of these to reach Chip was Greg Moran.

FIELD HOUSE RECORD

"Great, Chip! Great! You broke the scoring record. Congratulations on the win, too! I'll wait for you right here after the game. Going to the station with you."

The photographers and newsmen were next and walked along with him to the State dressing room. There the players staged another celebration. "Now we're on our way!" "Nice going, Bitsy!" "Yea, Speed!" "Some backhand shot, Chip!" "Atta boy, Sky!"

Sky Bollinger was the most enthusiastic. "Boy, would I have been ruined, or *would* I have been ruined, if Chip hadn't made that shot? Imagine him passing up a chance to win the game and break the record all on one play and giving me the ball! Guess you guys would've made me walk home if he hadn't made it!"

"It worked out all right," Chip said gaily. "Forget it!"

The newspaper writers were still typing their stories at the scoring table when Chip finished dressing and got back to the court. Greg was talking to the timekeeper and Chip motioned him to come along. Chip didn't want to get involved with the writers again.

Chip ushered Greg into a cab with Speed and Bitsy and Sky, despite the protests of the driver. "We're little guys," Bitsy said lightly. The driver eyed Sky's six-nine inches doubtfully but couldn't resist Bitsy's exuberance and smilingly acquiesced.

On the way, Greg took part in the conversation so easily and naturally that one would have thought he was an old friend. "What a comeback! You sure caught us by surprise."

"We had Southwestern going, too," Sky said. "Or, rather, Chip did."

"We'll get 'em the next time!" Speed added.

"If you play as you played tonight," Greg agreed. "They're tough, though. Tonight was game number forty-three and they've got three more before the tournament. Coach Habley believes in keeping them busy."

"When do they go to school?" Sky asked.

"Probably on the train," Greg replied, laughing.

They arrived at the depot, then, and Jimmy was waiting. He greeted Greg warmly and the three friends left the others and went across the street for a milkshake and a sandwich. Jimmy and Greg talked about their high school experiences. Chip listened and said nothing about his resolve to get Jimmy back in school. When he got on the train he shook hands with his two friends and promised to write. The look in Jimmy's eyes was still with him when he went to bed and he couldn't sleep; he couldn't get Jimmy's problem out of his mind and tossed until daylight.

When the train pulled into University at eight o'clock Thursday morning, Chip was tired out, but he had worked out a plan to get Jimmy back on the basketball team and back in school. He could hardly wait to get started on the plan and hurried to Pete's restaurant his first free period. Pete welcomed him warmly.

"Hiya, Chip. Wonderful win last night. Just readin' about the game here in the paper. Boy, you did yourself proud! Fifty-five points! Wow!" His happy expression changed. "See Jimmy? How is he?"

"He's fine, Pete, but his heart is just about broken. Listen, I've got an idea. Thought about it all night. Jimmy's father is sick and won't be back in the restaurant for a week or so, maybe longer. Tommy

Lu Chung is a good restaurant man. Jimmy says he is an expert in American food. . . .

"How is this for an idea? Suppose we could get the restaurant on a paying basis and could get Tommy back on the job to take charge? Then, Mr. Lu Chung might be willing to let Jimmy come back to school. He might even let him play in the tournament. Sound all right?"

Pete's eyes brightened. "Sounds good! You sure Jimmy would go along with the scheme?"

"He hasn't said so, but I think he will. Especially if Tommy will come home and help."

"You think the old man would let Jimmy come back to school?"

"Yes, I do. Education and all kinds of learning are especially important to the Chinese, Pete."

"Well, count on me! Where do we start?"

"I can't get away from school and practice, and that's where you come in. If you can get Tommy down here, so we can talk to him, we will be able to find out what we need and where to start. Jimmy says Tommy has a lot of wonderful plans for the restaurant and that was the reason he left home."

"You got the address? Good! You know what I'm going to do? I'm goin' to get in my car right now and drive to Chicago and bring that fellow back with me, dead or alive! It's only a four-hour drive. I'll have him back here tomorrow. If he's any kind of a brother at all he'll be glad to help Jimmy. You want action? You got action! Right?

"Now listen, Chip. Jimmy is important to Pete's Place. Jimmy is important for his own sake, but he's also important to the business. See you tomorrow and I'll have Tommy Lu Chung with me. By lunchtime! Positively!"

Pete was back at noon on Friday, and Tommy Lu Chung was with him. "All set, Chip. Meet Tommy. He quit his job. If this idea of yours doesn't click, he's going to work for me."

Tommy was about as tall as Jimmy but not as well put together. But he had the same brown, steady eyes and friendly expression. Pete had evidently briefed his passenger thoroughly and Tommy was ready and willing.

"I want to do my part," he said, spreading his hands. "If Jimmy needs help, I'm ready. However, it's a big job."

"You don't know me and Chip!" Pete boasted.

Tommy smiled briefly. "I know my father," he said significantly. "He's an extremely decided man."

"But he'll change if we can get the business to booming, won't he? That's the big problem facing the family right now, isn't it?"

Tommy nodded. "That is the most vital problem, yes. But there are other family matters which present difficulty, too."

"What's the next move?" Pete asked impatiently. "We haven't got much time."

"Right," Chip agreed. "The next thing is for you and Tommy to talk everything over and agree on the changes in the restaurant setup which will be needed and what the cost will be."

Tommy shook his head vigorously. "Few changes will be necessary. It is mostly the need for a change of policy. The location is excellent, the outside of the building can be fixed with a little paint, and the dining room requires nothing but some white paint to cover up all the colors of the rainbow which are on the walls."

FIELD HOUSE RECORD   137

"How about the kitchen equipment?"

"It is excellent," Tommy said proudly. "The ranges and tables and ovens and refrigerators are as good as you will find anywhere. And the kitchen is large and clean. No improvements are needed there."

"What about changing the name? Won't that be important?"

"Definitely! I've been thinking about a name for a long time and I think we should change to the New Campus Inn because we're located right off the Tech campus."

"Now what?" Pete asked impatiently.

"Well," Chip said, "Christmas vacation starts tomorrow. If you and Tommy can be ready, Soapy and I can take the one o'clock train for Clinton after the game tonight. Can you make it, Pete?"

"Sure! I'm in this all the way. I'll be ready."

"Good. Suppose you and Tommy talk everything over this afternoon and we'll complete our plans on the train."

"That's the kind of action I like," Pete said. "Tommy can help me this afternoon and go to the game with you tonight. Another thing. This extra traveling is going to cost you and Soapy a lot of money. I'll finance that item and figure it's money well spent if we can get Jimmy back. O.K. with you?"

"That's not necessary, Pete. We'll make it someway."

"You'll make it my way. And with my money! It's an investment."

Chip arrived early for practice that afternoon. It was an unusual procedure for the day of a game, but Coach Corrigan felt it was necessary because the players were leaving for their Christmas vacations right after the game that night. Rockwell was on hand with mimeographed scouting reports of the teams that had been invited to the tournament and these were distributed and discussed.

Corrigan talked afterward about the game with Cathedral that night and finished with an outline of their plans for the tournament. "We'll report back here for practice on Thursday, December 23, and leave that night for Clinton. Keep in shape next week in a gym if you can, but if that is impossible, do some roadwork. Now let's take Cathedral tonight and then start thinking about winning the tournament."

After the practice, Chip hurried down to the locker room and cornered Murph Kelly. "Don't give Jimmy Lu Chung's uniform to anyone else and be sure to pack it for the tournament. I'm going to have him back in time to play."

Chip had lots of things to do that afternoon. He met Soapy and urged him to pack that afternoon. "We won't have much time after we close up tonight."

"Why? Where we going?"

"Clinton! Tonight! You and Pete and Tommy Lu Chung and I are going into the restaurant business. For a few days, anyway!"

CHAPTER 15

PURPOSE OF THE INVASION

University is a regular stop for the Midnight Main Liner going east and the conductors, brakemen, porters, and waiters are used to the student turmoil which greets them at the start of school vacations. Hundreds of State students had remained in University to see the Statesmen win from Cathedral, 74 to 69, and they were in a gay mood. The name of Chip Hilton was on the lips of many of the basketball fans as they talked about State's third straight victory and the thirty-six points the blond bomber had scored for the winning cause.

Many of them wandered up and down the aisle of the car in which Chip and Soapy and Tommy and Pete sat, without recognizing the player who had sparked the victory and scored nearly half of his team's points. Perhaps it was because the foursome was so seriously engrossed in discussing the price of beef, chicken, eggs, butter, cheese, vegetables, and fish.

Chip had been "hot" again and had scored thirty-six points in twenty-nine minutes. But as soon as the game was over he had plunged right back into the problem of the New China Tea House. And he was right back at it as soon as they found seats on the train.

"Greg Moran is meeting us at the station in the morning and then we're going to get Jimmy in a huddle and get started. I worked out a job assignment for each of us yesterday afternoon."

"It is a big step for Jimmy," Tommy said thoughtfully. "It will be necessary for him to discuss the plans with our father. Right now, it's important that I present humble self to my father and beg his forgiveness for my long absence."

None of Tommy's listeners attempted to advise Tommy with respect to his family obligations and shortly afterward each quieted and tried to get as much sleep as possible.

The train pulled into the Clinton station right on time at seven o'clock in the morning and Greg Moran was waiting. Greg knew Tommy slightly and shook hands, and then Chip introduced him to his other friends and explained the purpose of the invasion. "We're out to get Jimmy back in school and on the team and we need your help."

"You've got it. What can I do?"

"Nothing right now, but we'll all get together just as soon as Tommy has seen Jimmy and his father. We're to meet them at the Chinese-American Club at two o'clock. Where can we get some reasonable lodgings?"

"The Moran house is the best place in town," Greg said, laughing. "Move in with us. We have lots of room."

Chip vetoed that and they settled for the Wilson Tech Campus Hotel. Tommy accompanied them to

PURPOSE OF THE INVASION 141

the hotel and then cut across the campus to the New China Tea House, and Greg went home to borrow the family car. Greg showed up shortly before two o'clock and drove them to the Chinese-American Club where Jimmy and Tommy were waiting in front of the building.

The car emptied and they surrounded Jimmy, shaking his hand and making a fuss over him. Jimmy was upset. Despite his hearty welcome, Chip could sense it in his eyes and in his voice. But the plan had gone too far to draw back now and Chip took the initiative. "How's your father?"

"He's pretty sick, Chip. I guess he won't be able to work for a long time."

"Tommy tell you about our plan?"

"Yes, Chip. I don't know what to do."

"Only one thing to do! You're the head of the family, now, and it's your responsibility to take care of the business. You're supposed to make it a success, right?"

"Yes . . ."

"All right! I've got everything planned. We start Monday on the outside, painting and changing the name. Everyone gets a paintbrush and pitches in. Pete is in charge of that. On Tuesday we clean up the inside and cover all the different colors with white paint. Pete is in charge of that, too."

"But where is the money coming from?"

Pete elbowed Soapy and Greg back a pace, and then, with elaborate gestures, pulled a huge roll of bills out of his pocket. "Look," he said grandiloquently, "this is where the working capital is coming from. And if we need more, I can get it!"

"But maybe we can't pay it back."

"No *buts!* You don't have to pay it back unless

this plan of Chip's goes over. If it doesn't, I'll charge the whole thing up to experience."

"It isn't going to cost much," Chip added. "Now, Greg and I are going to work out a sales plan and the advertising program—"

"Excuse me, Chip," Greg interrupted, "I can really help in that department. It's a pipe! Toots Chandler is the school's publicity director and he's engaged to my sister. He'll do anything I say. He knows every sports writer in town!"

"That's great!" Chip said quickly.

"And," Greg continued, "he can get us a break on the sports pages and that will fall right in line with your plan to make the New Campus Inn the sports center of Clinton."

"Sports center?" Jimmy echoed weakly.

Chip nodded quickly. "Sure! Coach Rockwell told me he would arrange for State to set its training table up here and that means over a hundred dollars a day income right there. Then we can work on the other teams and line them up for the same thing."

Greg laid a hand on Chip's arm. "Sorry, Chip. Don't like to be butting in all the time, but Toots has charge of arranging the quarters and meals for all the teams and he'll be tickled pink to have a place so close to the campus. I'll call him right now, O.K.?"

"And how!" Chip assented. "On your way!"

"Wait a minute," Soapy chimed in. "How about tickets to shows and radio programs and things like that? Couldn't the New Campus Inn be the center for handing out the Annie Oakleys to the teams and players?"

"Sure!" Greg said. "Toots is loaded with them.

Don't worry about that! Keep talking. I'll be right back!"

Chip carried on again. "You and Tommy and Pete will do the buying and set up the kitchen. Soapy will have to get a staff to wait tables, even if he has to use Biggie Cohen and Red Schwartz and every State student from Valley Falls and Chet Stewart's Big Red high school basketball team. And it won't cost anything except their meals. "Don't worry. You can't miss! We're not going to let you miss!"

"But—"

"No *buts!* Now you and Tommy go back home and tell your father you've got some new ideas and you're sure they will make money."

Jimmy nodded uncertainly. "All right, Chip. Er— could Tommy and I speak to you privately?"

"Sure. Come on, I'll walk you part way home. Wait here for Greg, Soapy—Pete. I'll be right back."

As soon as they were out of earshot, Jimmy began. "Chip, I'm worried sick about this whole thing. Pop wouldn't talk to Tommy this morning and Tommy doesn't know what to do. He's thinking about going back to Chicago. Then there's the restaurant. Pop is dead set in his ways and ideas . . ."

"I know, Jimmy. But this is the chance you and Tommy both have wanted. And with all the help we've got, I'm sure it will go over the top. If it doesn't, there won't be much loss. You're losing money now. Why not try it?

"As far as Tommy is concerned, I think he should stay here and show his father what he can do. Then, if it doesn't go over and you can't come back to school, Tommy can take your place with Pete."

Chip gripped Jimmy tightly by the arm. "Tommy deserves a chance, too. This is it."

"All right," Jimmy agreed reluctantly. "We'll give it a try."

Chip could scarcely restrain a shout of relief. "Good. We've got a week before the teams arrive for the tournament and another ten days before school begins. You haven't resigned from State, yet, so you're still on the rolls as a student and you're still eligible for basketball."

"Might as well forget the basketball," Jimmy said shortly. "All I hope is that *you* get another chance at Southwestern."

Chip explained that Soapy and he had to go on home that afternoon, but that they would be back Monday morning ready to go to work. "Pete is staying over. He'll meet you at the restaurant tonight. He's a good man and knows the business. Guess I don't have to tell either of you that . . ."

Chip, Soapy, Pete, and Greg spent the rest of the afternoon going over further plans for the New Campus Inn and by train time had covered every detail. Greg was enthusiastic and promised to get half of the girls in school lined up for Chip's telephone campaign. "I can get a lot of girls to work, too," he said enthusiastically. "I know just about every waitress in school," he boasted. "Most of them are local girls and won't be doing anything until school starts. Don't you worry about that little detail."

"Only two restrictions," Soapy warned. "They've got to work and they've got to be beautiful."

On the train, Chip settled himself comfortably in his seat, anticipating a good rest during the ten-hour trip. But Soapy was curious and wide awake

PURPOSE OF THE INVASION 145

and full of questions. "What's this telephone campaign Greg was talking about?"

"We're going to make lists of people for the girls to call and tell about the New Campus Inn. Faculty, local students, societies, and all kinds of groups and organizations."

"Good idea. Say, most of the teams will be in Clinton for Christmas and New Year's. You figuring on anything special?"

"That's your department. Get busy and make some plans. I'm going to sleep."

Ten hours later, two tired boys alighted in a blinding snowstorm at the Valley Falls depot. There wasn't a taxi in sight. "True to form," Soapy grumbled. "C'mon. Might as well hit the trail. Gee, I'll never make it home in this. Guess I'd better stay at your house."

Mary Hilton was awake as soon as they stomped up on the porch, and she hurried downstairs and ushered them into the warm living room. Then she served hot tea and cookies, and shooed them off to bed after Chip outlined his plans to get Jimmy Lu Chung back in school. She was disappointed that Chip would not be home for the entire week, but she was in complete sympathy with his intense desire to help a friend.

Chip had a wonderful time the next day. He went to church in the morning with his mother, and after lunch got a ride with Speed Morris down to the Sugar Bowl. All the old crowd was there, on the sidewalk just outside the entrance. Most of them were curious about the tournament.

"You see the draw, Chip?" someone asked. "Petey pasted it in the window. State meets Dane in the first round. Know anything about them?"

146   TOURNAMENT CRISIS

"Not much," Chip said, moving up to the window to study the draw sheet.

"Gave A. & M. a bye, Chip," Speed said. "How come?"

HOLIDAY INVITATIONAL DRAW

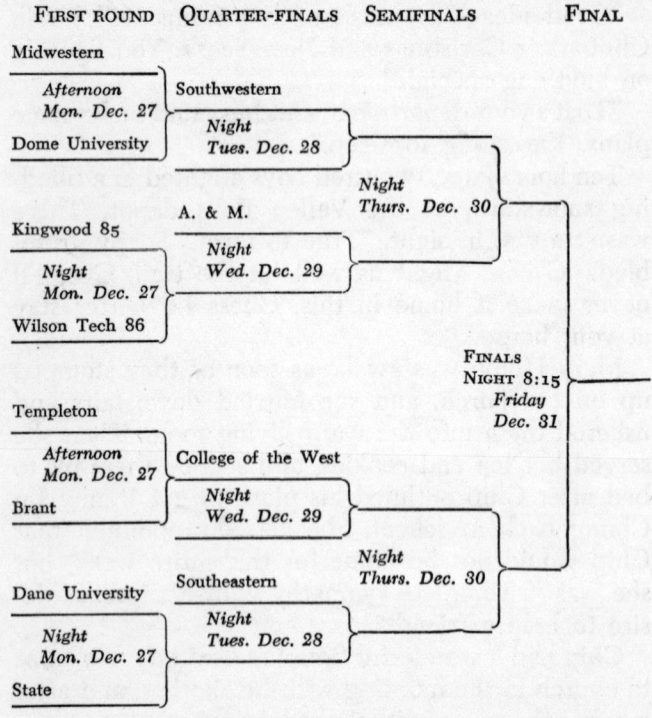

First round	Quarter-finals	Semifinals	Final

Midwestern
— *Afternoon Mon. Dec. 27* → Southwestern
Dome University
— *Night Tues. Dec. 28* →
— A. & M. — *Night Wed. Dec. 29* →
Kingwood 85
— *Night Mon. Dec. 27* →
Wilson Tech 86
— *Night Thurs. Dec. 30* →

Templeton
— *Afternoon Mon. Dec. 27* → College of the West
Brant
— *Night Wed. Dec. 29* →
Dane University
— *Night Mon. Dec. 27* → Southeastern
State
— *Night Tues. Dec. 28* →
— *Night Thurs. Dec. 30* →

**Finals
Night 8:15
Friday
Dec. 31**

Friday Afternoon, December 31: Semifinal Losers Play for Third Place
Seeded List: 1—Southwestern   2—College of the West
              3—A. & M.   4—Southeastern

"They were champions of the conference last year, Speed. Guess that's the reason. Hmmm, Dane . . . Rock said they played a possession game."

Speed pulled his copy of Henry Rockwell's scouting notes out of his pocket. "That's right," he added. "Play slow and make few mistakes. Got a big center. Six-ten and good."

"Southwestern is seeded number one," someone in back of Chip said. "They as good as everyone says? That's the only team anyone around here talks about."

"Yeah, Chip, you think it's the greatest team of all time?"

Chip swung about and faced the group. "Hold it," he said, laughing. "What am I supposed to be? How would I know whether or not it's the greatest of all time?"

"You played against them and you got twenty-five points—"

"Yeah," Speed interrupted, "and he got clocked, too! But good! It's a good team but they play dirty ball. No team is great that plays dirty!"

CHAPTER 16

A TEAM WITHOUT A WEAKNESS

Tommy Lu Chung had no experience with a paintbrush but the artistry in his hands worked wonders with the big sign hanging in front of his father's restaurant. By some miraculous means he had changed the carvings and the colorings on the sign until it looked as if it had been designed and wrought exclusively for the New Campus Inn.

Chip and Soapy arrived in Clinton at ten o'clock Monday morning and took a taxi direct to the restaurant. Tommy had completed the blue-and-gold sign by that time and was helping Jimmy and Pete and Greg on the front of the building. The newcomers sat in the cab, too surprised to move, and viewed the transformation. The frame structure had absorbed the first coat of white paint beautifully and the big sign with its gold-and-blue letters looked like a million dollars.

Pete spotted them from his high perch on a ladder and bellowed a greeting. "C'mon. We got work to do! Hope you brought some work clothes."

That shocked them to life and they paid the taxi driver and hustled to the front entrance. A sign announcing that the New Campus Inn was closed for alterations was tacked on the door. Inside, two men were installing a telephone. Chip and Soapy changed clothes in the checkroom and hurried out to join the workers.

"How's it look?" Pete demanded.

Before either could answer, Jimmy interrupted. "We're getting the telephone!"

"Greg's got the tickets all set," Tommy added.

"That's right," Greg said proudly. "Got some girls lined up to do the telephoning, too. They'll be here tomorrow afternoon. And, Chip, Toots thinks we ought to run ads in all the papers when we're ready to go. Another thing! He wants to get some classy menus printed up. He and Pete have started the design already. He'll be over tomorrow afternoon. Says we can count on practically all of the teams eating here."

'C'mon, you guys!" Pete growled. "We got two more sides to do and a second coat to put on. Today! Gotta get the outside all finished before sundown."

They did it! And then they started on the interior; piling up the tables and spreading newspapers over the floor and removing all the plants and other decorations. Chip was dead tired and Soapy and Greg were out on their feet. But they didn't quit. They tackled the ceiling with rollers dipped in soft blue paint and finished the job at midnight.

With the last roll of the paint in the center of the room—without a word, almost as if by command—they sat down on the floor and viewed the results of their labor. Then they looked at one another and burst into hysterical laughter. Hands and faces were spattered with blue and white paint and Soapy's hair had changed from a bright red to speckled blue.

They cleaned up as best they could and called it a day.

Tuesday saw real progress. They finished the dining-room walls before lunch and started on the woodwork. When Toots Chandler showed up, Chip stopped long enough to get acquainted and to outline his plans. Chandler proved as enthusiastic as Greg and assumed full responsibility for the menus, the publicity, and the designation of the New Campus Inn as the food center for the teams entered in the tournament.

"It's all laid on," he said quietly. "Another thing! The school is sponsoring a luncheon for the tournament sports writers and it's scheduled for Friday noon. The tournament treasurer will pick up the tab and it will give you a chance to sell the writers on the New Campus Inn. Can you handle it?"

Jimmy was nodding his head so emphatically that he nearly fell off the ladder on which he was standing. "Sure! We can handle it! And how!"

A little later the girls appeared and all work immediately ceased. This time Soapy nearly fell off the ladder. Greg introduced everyone and this time Chip had too much help. He explained that the idea was to make up a list of organizations, students, faculty, and persons who might be interested in special lunches or dinners. Then they were to be contacted by telephone and told about the New Campus Inn. Some of the girls were waitresses and these were referred to Tommy, since he was going to serve as headwaiter and banquet manager.

"How about me?" Soapy demanded. "I've got to have help with my project. I can't handle a big Christmas and New Year's party all by myself."

WITHOUT A WEAKNESS 151

"I can take care of that," Greg said. "Our cheerleaders would go for something like that in a big way."

Everything seemed to click, and when Chip and Soapy took the train back to University Wednesday night, the New Campus Inn was ready to open its doors for business on Thursday morning.

The staff was in fairly good shape. Pete's brother had taken over for him in the restaurant in University until the end of the tournament, and he and Jimmy were in full charge of the kitchen. A few of the old kitchen workers had returned when they saw the rejuvenated setup, and Tommy had selected a number of the student waitresses to help in the dining room.

The transformation was unbelievable and now the stage was set for the vital part of Chip's plan.

Chip and Soapy didn't do much talking on the train. They were sound asleep almost as soon as they hit the seats. When they reached University, Soapy said good-by and headed for State Drug to arrange for a substitute on the fountain until the end of the tournament. "I'm going back this afternoon and I'll meet you tomorrow morning at the station in Clinton."

Chip reported to Murph Kelly and was given a green light for practice. Corrigan drilled them until twelve o'clock and then excused them until three o'clock. Chip made it a point to tell Henry Rockwell what had been accomplished in Clinton. "He'll play," he said confidently. "Wait until Mr. Lu Chung finds out Tommy can handle the restaurant and sees the new plan in operation."

Chip took a nap in his room at Jeff and was refreshed and raring to go at the afternoon practice.

After the workout, he caught up on his work at State Drug. When he left, everyone gave him a royal send-off.

"Bring back that big cup!"

"Watch out for Southwestern!"

"We'll be watching you on television!"

Speed was waiting for him at Jeff, all packed, and eager to give him a hand. "It's a great feeling, Chipper. Imagine, we're in the big tournament."

Chip was busily pulling out bureau drawers and turning suit pockets inside out. Speed watched curiously.

"What are you looking for?"

"That clipping about Jimmy. The write-up about him in the Statesman."

"Maybe it's in one of your books."

Chip searched through his schoolbooks and found it in his Chinese history text. "Good! Had me worried."

"What are you going to do with that?"

Chip explained that it was an important bit of ammunition he was accumulating for Jimmy's father. "Going to be all ready for him," he said, grinning happily. "Let's go."

"This is going to be my first Christmas away from home," Speed said ruefully.

"Me, too," Chip said, "but it's worth it."

Soapy met them in Clinton the next morning and reported what had happened at the grand opening. "It was great, Chip—Speed. Never saw anything like it. Boy, this is going to be some day! If Jimmy's father isn't sold on this deal, he wouldn't even appreciate the Pump Room in Chicago. . . . Oh! You oughta see Greg and me in our white coats. We're Tommy's junior headwaiters. Some fun!"

WITHOUT A WEAKNESS

It *was* fun. But it was for keeps, too. The faces of Jimmy and Tommy showed the strain, but there was happiness in their eyes and in their voices when they greeted Chip. Coach Corrigan, Rockwell, and the State team arrived early and were given a special table in a corner of the room. Sports writers were standing around in small groups, talking to players and coaches from the different teams. Chip excused himself and went to look for Pete. He found him in the kitchen, working away, quietly and efficiently. Pete grunted a welcome and kept right on going.

Jimmy and Tommy stopped their work for a second and Jimmy clutched Chip's arm and shook him gently. "Business is great, Chip. I think it's going to work."

"I've always dreamed of this," Tommy said enthusiastically. "You're a genius, Chip."

"That's a laugh."

"I mean it. It was your ideas and your perseverance and determination that sold us. We'll never forget it."

"How's your father?"

"Much better. He expects to come to work the first of the week."

"Could I see him before Monday?"

"I'm afraid not, Chip. It wouldn't be wise."

"Then I'll see him here the first thing Monday morning."

When Chip returned to the dining room, several other teams had arrived and Toots Chandler was introducing coaches and writers and players. After lunch, the teams remained seated and various coaches were called upon to talk about their teams and the tournament. And while they were speaking, the customers kept piling in.

Corrigan wanted to talk to Jimmy, and Chip took him out in the kitchen. Jimmy was embarrassed. "I'm sorry I had to leave without seeing you, Coach, but I couldn't help it."

"By the looks of this, it's understandable, Jimmy. But you're still on the team and we're counting on you to play. Can you make practice this afternoon? We really need you. We want to win this tournament and you can help us do it."

Jimmy shook his head regretfully. "It's impossible while my father is ill."

"Chip tells me he may be back on the job on Monday. That won't be too late."

"I wish I could feel as confident as Chip," Jimmy said, smiling gently. "I don't know what I would have done without him."

"I don't know what we'd do without him, either," Corrigan said, smiling and slapping Chip on the back. "Well, we'll be pulling for you, Jimmy, and just as soon as your father gives his O.K., come running!"

That afternoon and night was a bewildering experience for Chip. So many things happened that he couldn't keep track of anything. State practiced and there was the inevitable posing for pictures and interviews with the writers and then watching the other teams practice and back to the New Campus Inn. Then there were tickets for the Friday night boxing show, and bed. Chip called his mother just before he went to bed to wish her Merry Christmas. After he finished the call he turned out the light and was still trying to remember all the things which had happened since last Monday when he fell asleep.

Saturday was worse. It was Christmas Day and

WITHOUT A WEAKNESS 155

the holiday spirit added to the excitement. The New Campus Inn was jammed all day. In the afternoon, after the big turkey dinner, the players who weren't practicing met at the restaurant to watch the game between Southwestern and College of the West in Chicago on television. Toots Chandler had located the set somewhere and it had been installed for the pleasure of the athletes.

Several writers joined the group and entered into the spirit of the rejuvenation of the New Campus Inn. "What's the big idea?" they queried. "What happened to the Tea House?" "Whose idea is this?" "Why all the help from the college kids?"

But those in the know were saying nothing and that added to the suspense and the fun of the whole experience.

Meanwhile, the game was on the screen and several strangers were keeping notes on the tables. "This could be a preview of the finals right here next Friday night," someone said.

Soapy couldn't take that. "Except for one thing," he said. "State will be one of the teams."

"State? They haven't got the horses, sonny. It's a one-man team. Haven't got a thing except Hilton."

"Haven't got the horses, my eye! Rack this up . . . in your hat! State will outrun and outshoot any team in the country. Wait and see!"

"I'll wait . . ."

The action of the game was on the screen, then, and the conversation stilled except for occasional remarks. "They're a rough outfit."

"You see that? Wasn't that a foul?"

"Things look different on television."

Chip concentrated on the screen, oblivious to the remarks, anxious to verify the weakness he suspected

—Southwestern's inability to play a wide-open, slam-bang, individual game. . . .

It was a rough game to work and the officials barely held it in check. College of the West was one of the best teams in the country and gave Southwestern a fight. But the champions had too much poise and won by a score of 78 to 71.

The announcer summarized the scoring and concluded with a resumé of Southwestern's season. "So—fans—Southwestern winds up its pre-tournament season with a great string of forty-seven straight victories over a two-year period. The Holiday Invitational Champions will be seeking their forty-eighth victory Tuesday night at Clinton when they take top billing in the feature game. Every ticket for this night has been sold out for weeks. The preliminary game brings together Southeastern, seeded number four, and the winner of the Monday night game between Dane University and State, seeded sixth and tenth respectively—"

That broke up the afternoon excitement and Chip and Soapy joined Jimmy and Tommy in the kitchen. The brothers were studying a sports page. "See this, Chip?" Jimmy asked. "See this write-up on Southwestern?"

WILSON TECH COACH LAUDS CHAMPIONS:

Southwestern Team Without a Weakness

Clinton, Dec. 25 (AP).—Southwestern figures to become the first team to win the Holiday Invitational Tournament five times in a row, now or ever.

Southwestern plays College of the West in Chicago this afternoon and then board an airplane for Clinton where they are confident of stretching their successive winning streak (providing they win this afternoon) to fifty straight at the expense of at least three teams in the Holiday Invitational and repeat last year's triumph in the process.

No Weakness

"Southwestern is a team without a weakness," Bill Todd, Wilson Tech coach, declared yesterday while preparing his Technicians for the tournament. Coach Jeff Habley has welded five great stars into an organization which carries the mantle of greatness as naturally as most teams wear warm-up jackets."

Habley and his twelve-man varsity squad will arrive in Clinton tonight and will taxi directly to the Green Acre Country Club. The team will work out Monday morning at the WT field house and it's a shame the tournament committee didn't think of charging admission to the practice. It would be a sellout!

"Well?" Jimmy demanded.

"It's a great write-up," Chip said, choosing his words carefully. "And Southwestern's a great team. But we can beat them." He paused, eyed Jimmy appraisingly, and continued slowly, "Some team is going to beat Southwestern, Jimmy, and I want to play on the team that does it. We're all counting on you to help us do it . . ."

Jimmy swallowed hard. "I'd do anything for you and the team, Chip. You know that! But a person of Chinese ancestry has responsibilities an American can't understand . . ."

Tommy hadn't said a word. Now he struck his fist sharply on the table and eyed Jimmy fiercely. "An *American* can't understand?" he echoed. "When you speak of an American you are speaking of yourself. When will *you* learn that America is your country and not China? You were *born* in America! *Not* in China! You're an *American!*"

CHAPTER 17

HAVE A FRIEND—BE A FRIEND

SOAPY'S CHRISTMAS PARTY was a great success. The Tech cheerleaders, boys and girls, had gotten behind the affair and had rounded up all the sorority girls who lived in and near Clinton to act as hostesses. Toots Chandler, who believed in big-time promotions, succeeded in getting the Tech Tournament Committee to finance the hiring of an orchestra and the cost of supper snacks for the guests of honor —the tournament players. Soapy and Greg acted as hosts, introducing the players one by one under the spotlight, and then kept busy introducing the girls to the boys. Jimmy and Pete and the kitchen staff were bustling about preparing sandwiches and salads and supper snacks, which were served by Tommy's staff of girls.

Chip watched the dancing until ten o'clock and then went back to the hotel and to bed. But it took him a long time to go to sleep. His heart was filled with thoughts of the great friendships he had made and the sacrifices such fellows as Pete and Greg and Toots Chandler were making for a friend who needed help. And then he thought of the wonderful

HAVE A FRIEND—BE A FRIEND 159

spirit of the Tech fellows and girls who had pitched in to help their friend, Greg Moran. Chip wasn't sure of the wording, but he *was* sure that the actions of all the people who had worked to make the New Campus Inn a success must prove the old axiom that to have a friend, a fellow had to be a friend. And that was what he was still thinking about when he fell asleep.

Greg Moran took Chip and Soapy and Speed to church Sunday morning and that afternoon Coach Corrigan and Henry Rockwell held a two-hour skull practice. Rockwell had prepared mimeographed scouting notes on all the teams in the bottom half of the draw sheet, but he devoted most of his remarks to their first opponent, Dane University. "We'll take 'em one at a time," he said, smiling confidently.

Coach Corrigan interrupted him for a moment. "Fellows, Rock has notes on every team in the tournament. Naturally, both of us will see every game and try to get as much information as possible on the teams we're going to beat. But . . . we both think you should do your own scouting. So, we'll expect you to be at every game played by the teams in our bracket. O.K., Rock."

"That's right, fellows," Rockwell added. "In order to do a little better job, it might be wise for you to concentrate on individual players—players you may be matched up against. Study his face, shirt number, and his personal techniques. For example: Does he turn his head on the defense? Does he play his opponent or the ball? Does he try for interceptions? Does he switch well? When and where does he foul? Some players never foul an opponent until they are sure he is going to shoot.

"Now on the offense: Does he shoot from outside,

160 TOURNAMENT CRISIS

beyond the outer half of the free-throw circle? Does he dribble a lot? Is he a good passer? From what area on the court does he score? What does he do *without* the ball? Does he screen, pick, set up blocks? Is he a basket hanger? What does he do in the fast break . . .

"There's a lot more but that gives you a pretty good idea what to look for. Coach Corrigan and I will scout the offense and defense and special team tactics. Any questions?"

Rockwell then explained briefly that Brant used a zone and the fast break; Templeton played possession and used a weave and block attack; Southeastern, seeded fourth in the tournament, was small but extremely fast and well conditioned.

"We won't worry about the number two team, College of the West, right now," he said in conclusion. "We've seen them on television and we'll see them again Wednesday night."

After dinner Chip spent an hour at the New Campus Inn with Pete and Jimmy, and went back to the hotel to study the scouting notes. He was still studying them when Jimmy and Tommy paid him a surprise visit. "We just finished," Jimmy said. "What a week!"

"What a business!" Tommy said proudly. "We've taken in more money in the last four days than we used to take in during a whole month. Pop is going to get a pleasant surprise!"

"I hope, I hope," Jimmy added, his voice filled with anxiety and hope. "Anyway, this time tomorrow we'll know."

Every team in the tournament had arrived by Monday morning and all except Southwestern showed up for their meals at the New Campus Inn.

HAVE A FRIEND—BE A FRIEND

The champions were billeted at the Green Acre Country Club, a few miles out of the city.

Coach Corrigan called another skull practice in the morning, and as soon as it was over, Chip and Speed headed for the restaurant for lunch. "It's now or never," Chip said hopefully.

"Everything's going to be all right," Speed assured him.

The New Campus Inn was buzzing. If the ring of the cash register was any criterion of the success of his eldest son's business acumen, Li Lu Chung could do nothing less than capitulate and back Jimmy's bid for basketball honors and a college education.

Jimmy and Tommy were both scared. Chip could see it in their eyes and in the furtive manner in which they watched the door. Tommy was hovering by a window overlooking the street and was the first to see his father. He rushed back to the kitchen where Chip was setting up trays for Jimmy and Pete. "Here he comes! Heaven help us!"

Chip followed Jimmy and Tommy out of the kitchen and sat down beside Soapy at the State table. He recognized Mr. Li Lu Chung as soon as he entered the door. The resemblance between the father and his two sons was remarkable.

Li Lu Chung's shoulders were broad and his posture was almost poker-stiff. It made him appear taller than Jimmy or Tommy. He wore a dark, double-breasted suit, a dark tie, and a gray hat with a dark band. His face was broad, with high-arched eyebrows, and his thin lips were pinched tight together. He paused in the door and Chip imagined he saw a quick intake of breath as Li Lu Chung surveyed the busy scene. Then Jimmy

162 TOURNAMENT CRISIS

and Tommy reached his side and bowed from the waist.

Chip could not hear what was being said, but there was no change in Mr. Li Lu Chung's expression. He bowed and said something, then walked slowly toward the office. Chip noted that the keen brown eyes were focused straight ahead, but he was sure Mr. Li Lu Chung made mental notes of every face and every detail in the room and catalogued it for future reference.

Jimmy and Tommy followed their father, almost as sober-faced. Tommy brought up the rear and as

Then Jimmy and Tommy reached his

HAVE A FRIEND—BE A FRIEND 163

side and bowed from the waist

he passed Chip he paused. "He's pleased," he whispered sibilantly.

"Then get it over with," Soapy whispered hoarsely.

"You don't know my father," Tommy retorted quickly. "He spends much time and sober thought before making a decision." He hesitated and then concluded, "If I can only get him to look at the receipts . . ."

It was a long wait. Chip, Speed, and Soapy had been served but they were not in an eating mood. Soapy sat facing the office door and kept up a rapid-fire flow of words. "Well, come on! What're they doing? Bet they're counting the money! Wish I could be in there for a sec. I'd straighten this thing out just like that." It seemed like an hour but it was little more than ten minutes later when Jimmy appeared. Alone!

It wasn't necessary to ask how he had made out. Jimmy's long face told the story. He sat down heavily in the chair beside Chip and ran his fingers nervously through his hair. Then his head dropped and he slumped forward.

"What happened?" Soapy demanded.

Jimmy sighed deeply. "Well, I told him the whole story," he said despondently. "And you know what he said? He said it was a trick; that I was thinking about basketball and not about my responsibilities as the eldest son. He said my place was here. More so, since I had so successfully demonstrated my ability to manage the business."

"Oh, brother!" Soapy managed, moaning deeply.

"How about Tommy?" Chip asked. "Didn't you tell him Tommy could take charge?"

Jimmy nodded. "Sure, Chip. But he wouldn't listen. Said it was my responsibility—not Tommy's."

HAVE A FRIEND—BE A FRIEND 165

"Well, I guess that's that," Soapy said. His voice was tired and all of his spirit and drive was gone.

"I really thought it would work," Jimmy said, rising slowly to his feet. "And I'm terribly sorry, after you have all worked so hard. I—I guess that's about all I can say." He walked along beside Chip and Speed and Soapy, and paused on the street just outside the entrance.

"How about coming to the game tonight?" Chip asked gently. "We're playing the second game."

"Thanks, Chip," Jimmy said in a low voice. "I'd better— Oh, there's my grandpop. I wonder what brings him down here. He seldom leaves the house Come on. I want you to meet him."

"Your grandpop?"

"Sure. He's a wonderful man."

Chip grabbed Jimmy by the arm. "You mean he's your father's dad?"

"Sure! Come meet him."

Chang Lu Chung was tall, very straight, and very thin. He had a thin face and wore a brown, pointed mustache and a short Vandyke beard. But it was his eyes which attracted Chip. The alert, brown eyes twinkled at their approach.

Jimmy bowed low and murmured, "Most honorable grandfather."

Chang Lu Chung acknowledged Jimmy's presence with a short bow and glanced at Chip. Chip bowed self-consciously. "Most venerable grandfather," Jimmy continued, "this is my beloved friend, Chip Hilton. And these other gentlemen are friends of Chip— Soapy Smith and Speed Morris."

Chang Lu Chung bowed to each and extended a long, thin hand in greeting. "Pleased to meet friends of young grandson," he said in a low, pleasant voice.

"I hope young grandson has been most gracious in his reception of his honorable friends, and it is my most humble desire to request a visit to our humble house when most convenient."

Chip and his pals acknowledged the greeting. Then, with a sympathetic glance at Jimmy, took their departure. Chip could hardly control his excitement. "I've got it!" he said, as soon as they were out of hearing. "Jimmy's grandfather! I forgot about Jimmy's grandfather! Jimmy's got a grandfather!"

Soapy gave Chip a sidewise glance, "Yeah, Chip, we know. Who hasn't?"

"You don't get it. Listen! You know those books I've been reading? Well, the whole of China's old civilization was woven out of the human relationships of father and son, older brother and younger brother. The family is the big thing and the descent of influence and power in the family stems from the eldest down— No matter how old another member of the family may be. Get it?"

Soapy was confused. "Nope, I don't."

Chip explained patiently. "The eldest son in this case is Jimmy's father and the patriarchal father of the whole Lu Chung family is Jimmy's grandfather. Get it now?"

Soapy got it! "Sure!" he said excitedly. "I get it! The grandfather, the old guy with the beard is the boss. We've been working on the wrong guy!"

"Right!" Chip said. "Jimmy told me one day that his father had never shown him any affection, always treated him like a man. Well, you just heard him say what a swell person his grandfather was and how he was always making a fuss over him. We had that in Chinese history. Anyway, the grandfather can lavish affection on the grandson that he can't show for his

HAVE A FRIEND—BE A FRIEND 167

own son. That explains the attitude of Jimmy's father."

Soapy nodded. "Right! Now what?"

"We've got to get to the grandfather. Jimmy's father has to do exactly what the grandfather says— Come on! I've got to think this out."

"It sure doesn't seem fair for Jimmy to have to go through all that medieval stuff at home and then try to be like us at school," Soapy said.

"It isn't fair, Soapy. But we've got to remember that it's not medieval stuff to them. We couldn't change that and we wouldn't want to. . . . It's just as real to them as our traditions are to us. Right now, our big problem is to make contact with Jimmy's grandfather."

"How about asking him to the game?" Speed suggested.

"It's got to be stronger than an invitation," Chip said thoughtfully. "Now if it was some sort of an obligation. You see, the Chinese feel that a debt of one member of the family is a debt of all. That's it! I'll get Jimmy to appeal to his grandfather from the point of view of a debt."

"You mean what we've done for the restaurant?" Soapy asked.

"Right! I'll phone Jimmy from the hotel and get him to put it up to his grandfather on that basis. You'll sit with him, O.K.?"

Soapy nodded emphatically. "And how!"

"You know something, Chip," Speed said tentatively. "We've been putting a lot of thought and work into getting Jimmy back on the team— What if we lose before we get him back?"

"We won't," Chip said grimly. "But if we do, isn't the real objective an education for Jimmy? Isn't the big thing getting Jimmy back in school?"

CHAPTER 18

BEYOND THE STARS TO REALITY

CHIP called the New Campus Inn on the telephone as soon as he reached the hotel and got Jimmy. "Hello! Jimmy? . . . Chip! Do you think you can get your grandfather to go to the game tonight? Soapy has tickets and can pick him up . . ."

Jimmy was downhearted and it took a lot of talking and urging before he would agree to talk to his grandfather. Before Jimmy would yield, Chip was forced to make some pointed references to what Jimmy's friends had done to put the New Campus Inn on its feet.

"All right, Chip," he said at last. "I'll call you right back."

Ten minutes later the telephone buzzed. It was Jimmy. "All set, Chip. My grandpop will be happy to attend the game." It was agreed that Soapy would pick Mr. Chang Lu Chung up at nine o'clock at the New Campus Inn.

"It's up to you now, Soapy," Chip said happily as he cradled the telephone. "Now, let's listen to the broadcast of the games."

There was a crowd of fifteen thousand fans present

to see the opening game of the tournament that afternoon. It was a close tense contest, but Dome passed Midwestern at the buzzer and won by a score of 73 to 71. In the second game, Templeton took the lead over Brant early in the first quarter and held it all the way to win 89 to 72.

"That narrows the field," Soapy said.

"I hope we can cut it down a little more!"

"You will! Guess I'd better get back to the restaurant."

Chip passed up the pregame meal and continued to rest. He had always shared Henry Rockwell's belief that the food an athlete ate just before a contest did nothing but slow him down. And when he came down in the elevator at eight o'clock he felt ready to play the game of his life. The lobby was crowded with fans and friends who had disdained the Kingwood–Wilson Tech game to escort their team to the game.

In the dressing room, Murph Kelly worked steadily, taping ankles quickly and efficiently. Word of the Kingwood–Wilson Tech game came filtering in by way of the State manager, Bill Jenkins, who was manning the State dressing-room door. It was a close fight but Tech pulled it out, 86 to 85. The score brought a smile to Chip's lips and he was happy for Greg and his teammates.

The big field house was jammed with fans when State trotted out on the floor. Chip took his turn in the warm-up and then located Soapy and Chang Lu Chung seated directly behind the State bench. Soapy caught Chip's eye and shook his fist over his head in a gesture of support. Chip could tell by the expression on Chang Lu Chung's face that he was amazed. He could see Soapy explaining the game. Gradually, Chang Lu Chung's face relaxed with keen enjoyment as he entered into the enthusiasm of the affair. Then he saw the old gentleman lean over and poke a long finger in Soapy's chest. Soapy was having a great time. He found Mr. Chang Lu Chung to be quick-witted, an apt sports student, and good fun.

"Young grandson would play here, too?"

"Sure," Soapy said. "He and Chip are teammates."

"Teammates are important to one another?"

"Yes, they are, Mr. Chung. It's something like the closeness of a family. One for all and all for one. They're important to one another and to their school. Teammates are like brothers."

Chang Lu Chung nodded. "I see. Young grandson is a good player?"

"He sure is! Everyone thinks State could win the championship if he could play." Soapy looked hopefully at his guest, but there was no indication that his words had any effect upon Chang Lu Chung. He was watching the game, concentrating on Chip.

Dane was a slow-moving team and the game was a terrific letdown after the action-packed preliminary. Coach Corrigan started co-captains Markley and Thornhill, Butcher King, Biz Gowdy, and Chip.

Early in the game, it was evident to everyone that King was in for a big night. His opponent was inches shorter and couldn't stop the Butcher's shots. But the Statesmen had difficulty in keeping up with Dane, even with King and Chip scoring freely. And once again it was evident that State was just an average ball club, despite the individual brilliance of Chip Hilton. The game was close all the way but the marksmanship of Chip and King was the difference. State won by a score of 73 to 70.

After the game, Coach Corrigan took the team to the New Campus Inn where the players enjoyed bulky steaks and all the trimmings. Jimmy was happy that State had won, but Chip could sense his friend's inner feeling of despair. Li Lu Chung was cool, concerned only with the welfare of the customers. But Chang Lu Chung enthusiastically recounted the events of the night to Jimmy and Tommy.

"It's working," Chip said, nudging Soapy. "Mr. Chang Lu Chung is interested. How did you do it?"

"Easy! Just told him about you and Jimmy. So far so good, but we'd better hurry up! The tournament will be over! What's the next step?"

"We'll wait for one more game. Jimmy said it was folly to rush him. He's our last hope."

"You can say that again. Jimmy's father is cold turkey. I don't think Mr. Chang Lu Chung can do anything with him either."

"Then I've been learning a lot of nonsense in my Chinese history class. Chang Lu Chung is the head of the family and will be as long as he lives. Li Lu Chung is the eldest son and that means Chang Lu Chung is the boss."

"O.K., Chip. I believe you. Only you guys better beat Southeastern or Jimmy will *never* get to come back to school."

The New Campus Inn was jammed all day on Tuesday and all of the Lu Chungs seemed happy with the rejuvenation of the restaurant. And that night when State lined up to face Southeastern, Soapy and Chang Lu Chung were again seated behind the State bench.

Southeastern was fast and liked to run. State couldn't keep up. Chip played sixteen of the twenty minutes in the first half but was limping badly at

172 TOURNAMENT CRISIS

the halfway mark. Southeastern led by a score of 48 to 44.

During the intermission, Murph Kelly worked exclusively on Chip's bad knee, and just before they returned to the court, held a short conference with Coach Corrigan. "Better give him a rest, Coach."

Corrigan was disappointed but he used Chip only four minutes of the third period, and it ended with Southeastern still leading by four points, 72 to 68. Chip had scored twenty-seven points during the twenty minutes he had played so far in the game.

But in the vital final quarter, the period in which games are won or lost, Coach Corrigan kept him in the full ten minutes. And it was a good thing he did, because it was Chip's sixteen points and last-second set shot which won the game for State by a score of 91 to 90. Chip limped all through the period and scored practically all of his points with outside shots.

After the game, when Chip and his happy teammates were in the State dressing room, the announcer gave a fast summary of the game. But the fans were so impressed by Chip's forty-three points in thirty minutes of play that their applause drowned out the rest of the State statistics.

Much as Chip would have liked to watch the Southwestern-Dome game, Murph Kelly prevailed, and he was sent back to the hotel to rest his knee. So Chip did not see the champions completely demoralize Dome and win easily by a score of 101 to 54.

Back at the field house, Soapy further amazed Chang Lu Chung by filling a notebook with circles and dots and dashes. "Scouting notes," he explained.

BEYOND THE STARS

"Scouting notes on the champions. On Southwestern. We're going to beat 'em in the finals!"

Chang Lu Chung pursed his lips and eyed Soapy doubtfully. "Big champions appear exceedingly superior. One would feel it necessary to suggest friend Chip and teammates have most difficult assignment."

A man seated next to Chang Lu Chung had been listening to the conversation. Now he ventured an opinion. "Impossible assignment is more like it."

"Oh yeah!" Soapy said quickly. "Wait and see."

"I believe you told me that once before," the stranger remarked. "At the New Campus Inn. Well, I'm still waiting."

"And we're still winning!" Soapy retorted. Then recognition dawned in his eyes. "Say, aren't you a scout?"

The stranger smiled. "I hope so. At least I'd better be. I'm the Templeton coach, Bill George."

"Then you musta been scouting State."

"Right again."

"But why aren't you scouting Southwestern?"

"Well, I know them pretty well. Enough to know no team in this tournament is going to beat them. You're star gazing."

"We'll beat 'em!" Soapy insisted. "We've got to beat 'em! We've got some vital reasons."

Coach George nodded understandingly. "You and a lot of other teams," he said dryly. "But you've got a couple of other teams to worry about first."

"You mean your own team, Templeton?"

"Right! College of the West, too."

Chang Lu Chung entered the conversation. "Star gazing is most restful to soul," he said blandly.

"But wise man looks beyond the stars to reality. Young friend is exceedingly wise gentleman."

"That's right," Soapy agreed proudly. "Ahem! Well, hope you whip College of the West. I'll be rootin' for you tomorrow night but you'll be rootin' for State come New Year's Eve!"

Coach George extended his hand. "I root for every team that plays against Southwestern, son. If Templeton isn't playing Southwestern Friday night for the championship, I sincerely hope it will be State. Good night to both of you and good luck."

Chip didn't lack for company after the game that night. Soapy took Mr. Chang Lu Chung back to the New Campus Inn and returned to the hotel with Speed, Murph Kelly, Henry Rockwell, and Coach Corrigan. And they brought a snack from Jimmy and Tommy and Pete Thorp. While Chip ate, they talked about the game and the conversation shifted to Southwestern and the possibility of Jimmy being able to play.

Soapy was gay and happy. "Two to go!" he gloated. "I can just see that big championship cup right now—sittin' on the fountain back at State Drug and me pourin' gallons of milk into it and then servin' every fan in town a big double frosted. Yum, yum!"

Coach Corrigan smiled, but he, too, was looking past the stars. "How about Jimmy?"

"That's right," Henry Rockwell added. "How are you making out with his father, Chip?"

"We're not making out. Soapy's trying to sell the grandfather, Mr. Chang Lu Chung, now. He's the patriarchal head of the family, even if he hasn't been working at it, and if Jimmy is going to have a chance to play, it's up to him."

"So that's who Soapy had in tow tonight," Coach Corrigan said. "Saw you in back of the bench, Soapy. How are you making out?"

"Mr. Chang Lu Chung will come around," Soapy answered, his voice expressing more confidence than he felt. "One more game, one more treatment, and he'll give us the restaurant."

"We don't want the restaurant," Rockwell said lightly. "We want to beat Southwestern. If we could be sure of Jimmy for that game we could be definite with our plans."

Corrigan nodded agreement. "That's right. Even if we had Jimmy for the semifinal game, I wouldn't want to use the press unless we couldn't win without it." He paused and, after a short silence, continued: "No, our objective is Southwestern and the championship. Just as Rock has so often said—we're taking them one at a time. But, in our hearts, each one of us has known ever since the Southwestern game that all our dreams were for another shot at the champions. A chance to square things."

"And," Rockwell added, "if we could count on Jimmy for the championship game, I believe it would give the team enough of a lift to get us by the semifinals Thursday night . . . whether we have to play Templeton or College of the West."

"Maybe so," Murph Kelly said, rising abruptly to his feet, "but it seems to me you're all overlooking a mighty important element. What if Chip's knee goes bad?"

CHAPTER 19

MOST VALUABLE PLAYER AWARD

CHANG LU CHUNG surprised both of his grandsons early Wednesday morning when he appeared at the New Campus Inn with an armful of papers all opened to the sports pages. "Young grandsons should be very proud," he said, spreading one of the papers on a table. "Be so good as to note that distinguished basketball friend is extremely important gentleman." A banner headline extended clear across the top of the page and Jimmy and Tommy read it avidly.

SOUTHWESTERN AND STATE GAIN SEMIFINALS

*Champions Win Easily—Crush Dome
State Edges Southeastern in Thriller*

Southwestern, the defending champion, seeded number one in the Holiday Invitational, scored an easy victory in the nightcap game last night to reach the semifinal round in the top half of the tournament bracket. In the preliminary, State made a dramatic last-minute surge to defeat Southeastern, 91–90, chiefly through the brilliant play of Chip Hilton. The star sophomore forward scored 43 points, although handicapped with a knee injury.

VALUABLE PLAYER AWARD 177

By its victory, Southwestern earned the right to meet the winner of tonight's A. & M.–Wilson Tech battle while State will face the victor of the Templeton–College of the West quarter-finals. Wilson Tech has surprised local fans by standing up through the tough competition of the tourney, and on the basis of the showing of both teams so far in the tournament, should best the Farmers. The Templeton–College of the West game is a tossup.

State, the Cinderella Team of the tournament, may have suffered a disastrous handicap last night. Chip Hilton, the Statesmen's scoring sensation, was favoring his right knee late in the game and may be slowed down for the semifinal contest slated for tomorrow night. Despite the injury, Hilton set this year's high scoring record, 43 points, and has averaged 35 points in each of the two games in which he has played. His season scoring total in eight games is 253 points in 202 minutes, or 1¼ points per minutes played.

Murph Kelly, State's veteran trainer, is concerned about the condition of Hilton's knee and expects Dr. Mike Terring, State's athletic physician, to arrive before the Thursday night game for a consultation. Kelly is especially thankful that his valuable charge will have nearly two days of rest before the semifinal test.

Southwestern had little trouble with Dome, and the champions should have no difficulty in sweeping through the coming tests to its fifth consecutive Invitational crown. College of the West, previously defeated by Southwestern, is probably best equipped to make the championship game a contest.

"Rubbish!" Jimmy said. "If Chip's knee is all right, he'll show 'em all by himself!"

"Eldest grandson greatly admires young friend?"

"Yes, reverend grandfather. He has done much for me and for our family. He is a true friend."

Chang Lu Chung nodded. "Distinguished young man looks beyond the stars," he said cryptically.

"Suggest honorable grandsons read further." He spread another paper on the table and pointed to a picture of Chip. "Young friend appears most certain of festival's greatest honor. Please note."

CHIP HILTON (STATE) LEADS FIELD FOR MVP

Chip Hilton, pictured above, racked up 43 points last night as he led State to a squeaker victory over Southeastern's gallant speedsters. It was a personal victory for the State scoring sensation and the brilliant sophomore continues to loom as a shoo-in for the Most Valuable Player Award. Hilton scored his 43 points in exactly thirty minutes of play . . .

"That's wonderful," Jimmy said happily. "Chip deserves all the credit in the world."

"What if he can't play?" Tommy asked.

"State won't win!" Jimmy said gruffly, turning quickly away.

Chang Lu Chung watched Jimmy walk toward the kitchen and then turned to Tommy. "Eldest grandson is extremely fatigued. Suggest he have some relaxation. You could manage restaurant alone tonight?"

Tommy nodded and grinned approval. And that was the reason Soapy was flanked by Chang and Jimmy Lu Chung when Templeton defeated College of the West, 52 to 49, and the home-town heroes, Wilson Tech, shaded A. & M., 87 to 83.

After the Tech game, Soapy tried to get Jimmy to join his former teammates at the hotel, but Jimmy was obdurate, and insisted he must hurry back to the restaurant. So the three friends walked back to the New Campus Inn where Tommy and Pete were waiting.

VALUABLE PLAYER AWARD 179

"Jimmy going to play or not?" Pete demanded, after Chang Lu Chung and Jimmy had walked into the office.

"We'll know tomorrow," Soapy said.

"If he isn't," Pete blustered, "I'm getting out of here!" He turned to Tommy. "What's the matter with your father?"

Tommy smiled understandingly. "My father is steeped in old-country customs, Pete," he said gently. "It takes more than just a few days to break down centuries of traditions. Be patient, please . . ." He turned and walked out in the dining room, leaving Pete and Soapy staring at the door.

"It will work out all right, Pete," Soapy said. "I'm going to talk to Mr. Li Lu Chung on my own tomorrow morning and Chip is just about ready to brace Jimmy's grandfather. Don't worry!"

Murph Kelly said Chip could accompany the team to the New Campus Inn for Thursday noon lunch. As soon as he reached the entrance, Chip knew something was wrong. The tables were crowded and Soapy was helping Tommy. But Soapy's freckled face was as red as a beet and he avoided the State table as if it didn't exist. Tommy disappeared into the kitchen and Jimmy immediately came out and sat down beside Chip, his face pale and worried.

"What's wrong with Soapy?" Chip asked.

"Pop," Jimmy whispered. "He's sick again. Early this morning Soapy asked him if I could play in the tournament. Pop blew up and started yelling in Chinese and poor Soapy didn't know what he was talking about. Pop was so excited that we had to send for the doctor. He's much better now and there's no danger, but Soapy is worried sick."

"I'd think so. Are you sure your father is all right? Is there anything I can do?"

"He's O.K., Chip. Honest! I wish you would try to explain to Soapy that it wasn't his fault. Pop always has those spells when he gets excited."

Chip followed Jimmy to the kitchen and took Soapy out in back of the restaurant. Soapy was a bundle of nerves, shaky and scared. "I'm sorry, Chip. I've ruined everything."

"Nonsense. What happened?"

"Well, I wanted to surprise you. I thought Jimmy's father would be so pleased about the restaurant that I could get him to let Jimmy play. So this morning I asked him, and he started yelling at me and had some kind of an attack and now he'll never let Jimmy play. And if anything happens to Mr. Lu Chung, it will be my fault."

"Nothing is going to happen to him. Jimmy says he's all right. Now you snap out of it."

It wasn't that easy. Soapy didn't snap out of it and Chip could do nothing about it. He and Speed went back to the hotel room but not to rest. Chip was worried about Soapy. Later, he called Jimmy and was relieved to find that Mr. Li Lu Chung was sitting up at home and was expected back at the restaurant the next day.

"He's more determined than ever that I can't play, Chip. In view of what happened this morning—"

"I know, Jimmy. We won't annoy him any more. By the way, is your grandfather there?"

"Yes, but—"

"Tell your grandfather I want to talk to him, will you, Jimmy? I'll be there in ten minutes."

"Are you crazy?" Speed demanded. "You'd better forget about Jimmy Lu Chung and rest your knee.

Haven't you done enough? Anyway, if we don't win tonight, it won't matter whether you talk to Chang Lu Chung or not."

"We'll see," Chip said patiently, pulling on his coat. "Now where's that clipping about Jimmy?"

"In the desk drawer. You're wasting your time, Chip. Heck, Jimmy couldn't blend in after such a long layoff, anyway."

Chip found the clipping and tucked it carefully in his pocket. "Jimmy could blend in with any team, Speed. Any day and any time so long as they used the press. He's always in shape and the press is made for him. We'll never beat Southwestern without him."

"You seem to be forgetting all about Templeton. We'll never beat them without *you!* And if we don't win tonight, nothing matters."

"That's where you're wrong. *Everything* matters. Besides, we're going to win tonight. Tell Rock I'll be back in time for skull practice. He knows where I'm going."

Jimmy and Tommy were waiting and ushered Chip into the office where their grandfather was reading a Chinese newspaper. When they entered the office, Chang Lu Chung bowed solemnly.

"Most happy to see young friend of grandsons," Chang Lu Chung said pleasantly. "Please be seated."

Jimmy and Tommy disappeared and Chip launched right into the subject, studying his host's face carefully as he spoke. "Jimmy deserves a chance to finish his education, Mr. Lu Chung. I've been studying Chinese history, and I know how vitally important education and learning are to the Chinese."

Chip hesitated and scanned Chang Lu Chung's face. There was no change in the inscrutable brown eyes and in the expression on the dignified face. "You see, Mr. Lu Chung," Chip continued, "Jimmy has told me about his father's home village in China and about all the changes which have taken place there. Jimmy feels that China will never again be the same as it was in the days of his father's youth."

Chang Lu Chung nodded. "That is so, my son," he said gently. "Continue, please."

"Jimmy loves America, Mr. Lu Chung, and he wants to build his future here. His heart is set on getting his college degree and following a career in science as an American."

Chip drew the newspaper clipping out of his pocket and placed it in the old gentleman's hand. "Jimmy is a fine student, Mr. Lu Chung, and I know that he didn't send this article home because he didn't want his father to know that he was playing basketball. But I think you should know of his accomplishments at State. This piece appeared in the school paper this month. Jimmy's professors all feel that he has a great future in the field of science, just as it says right there."

Chip paused again and studied Chang Lu Chung's calm and passive face, but, as before, there was no change. He continued slowly, "I hope you will think it over and help Jimmy. You may feel that the fellows and I helped Jimmy just so he could play on the basketball team. And that's true. But our *big* reason was to try to get the restaurant established so Jimmy could come back to school. And with Tommy doing such a wonderful job . . ."

"Jimmy is important to the team?"

"Yes, Mr. Lu Chung, he is. He's a wonderful player and he loves the game with all his heart."

Chang Lu Chung nodded. "Yes, that is not difficult to perceive. However, eldest grandson has certain family obligations which are far more important at the moment than the game of basketball or his presence at the college." He smiled and extended his hand graciously. "Good afternoon, young friend."

Chip left the office disheartened and low in spirits. He was glad that Jimmy and Soapy and Tommy and Pete were not in sight. He taxied back to the hotel and hurried up to the State conference room. Coach Jim Corrigan was chalking "press" notes on the portable strategy board when Chip slipped quietly through the door. Rockwell turned quickly and glanced hopefully at Chip, but the expectant light in his eyes faded when Chip shook his head.

Coach Corrigan paused, too. Then he continued: "Coach Rockwell has told you all we know about Templeton, and, as you know, we've been trying to save our special press for Southwestern. But if we have to use it tonight—well, we'll use it! Coach Rockwell and I feel it is the only type of game which can upset Southwestern. And that is the greatest sports desire I have ever experienced—to beat Southwestern. So we'll try to beat Templeton without the press. I think we can do it!"

His words were followed by a tight, tense silence, and the thoughts of most of the players in that room flashed back to the game in which they had been subjected to Southwestern's humiliating treatment.

"It is too bad Jimmy Lu Chung can't be with us. The method we use in applying the press is entirely new to the game, chiefly because of Jimmy's uncanny interceptive ability and skill in dribbling the ball and pulling the opponents out of position. Without

Jimmy, it's just another bit of strategy to use in an emergency. Nevertheless, if it's necessary, we'll give it all we've got.

"I know every person feels just as I do about Southwestern. I feel sure that feeling, the great desire we all possess, to get another chance at Southwestern will help us pull through tonight. A fighting team is hard to beat. . . .

"You're great fighters and I have never coached a more unselfish group. Coach Rockwell and I have been amazed time after time by your close-knit loyalty to one another, once you were welded into a team. That's what team sports are all about. Now, one more thing. Chip is limping around on a bad leg. Doc Terring will arrive just before game time to give Chip a final checkup. I hope he gives him a green light, but if he says Chip can't play—well, Chip will have to sit it out."

One could have heard a pin drop in the dead stillness which followed. Then Corrigan spoke again in the sharp, crisp tones he used in his coaching. "All right, now, Murph. A short walk around the block and then back to rest until six thirty. Any questions?"

There were no questions then or later. Coach Corrigan had said it all. Later, when the hotel waiters served the tense players toast and tea and jello in their rooms, Chip was sitting by the window, gazing far out over the city toward the New Campus Inn and thinking about Jimmy's fervent hopes and dreams for this night. And all at once Chip's spirits lifted and his heart sang with a great confidence. . . .

CHAPTER 20

THROUGH FOR THE TOURNAMENT

DR. TERRING prodded the knee with his sensitive and knowing fingers while his keen eyes noted the reaction in Chip's eyes. "Sure?" he asked. "Sure this doesn't hurt? Feels pretty tight to me." He glanced doubtfully at Chip again and then turned to Kelly. "All right, Murph," he said brusquely. "Suit him up!"

The watchful silence was broken as the players began tugging at suits and shoes, and Coach Corrigan and Henry Rockwell moved from player to player with words of encouragement and advice. Minutes later, State was out on the court, fired with a fierce determination to fight past Templeton and qualify for another chance at Southwestern. There wasn't a doubt in anyone's mind that the champions would take Tech in the second game.

Chip's knee was tight and he felt a slight twinge of pain as he trotted through the warm-up drill. But he covered up as best he could, knowing full well that Templeton's keen-eyed coach, Bill George, was watching every move he made. Behind the State bench, Soapy was seated alone, flanked on each side by two empty seats. It was Chip who clenched a fist this time and shook it encouragingly toward his pal. Then the referee's whistle shrilled and Chip followed his teammates over in front of the State bench and circled around Coach Corrigan and Henry Rockwell.

There were no last-minute instructions as the State players gripped hands. And it was the same in front of the Templeton bench. Coach George was surrounded by his players and they were just as quiet as they joined in a team clasp. Then the two teams lined up for the tap and Chip was gripping the hand of a tall, lean player who smiled as their hands and eyes met and said his name was Bill Johnson. Then the smile vanished and Johnson appraised Chip warily at close range.

Templeton got the tap and Chip dropped back on the defense, picking Johnson up as his tall opponent broke for the corner. Johnson broke right out again and then drove hard down the middle and it took all of Chip's speed to keep up with his opponent's long strides. Johnson had not yet touched the ball. He broke out again and once more cut for the basket at full speed.

Then Chip got it. . . . "Going to run me all night," he breathed to himself as his knee began to protest the frequent stops and turns and steady running. "Can't let on. Got to put up a good front."

Chip played it smart. He gave no evidence that the pace was too much for him, but he gave Johnson plenty of room. This cut down the distance he had to cover, but it also gave Johnson a chance for a clear shot and he took it. The ball never touched the rim and Templeton was out in front, 2 to 0. Coach Corrigan was on his feet as soon as the ball swished through the net and called time. Chip saw with dismay that Reb Tucker was moving toward

THROUGH FOR THE TOURNEY 187

the scoring table. "I'm all right, Coach," he protested.

"Don't worry about it," Corrigan said assuringly. "Rock and I have something up our sleeves, too."

Chip sat it out, groaning inwardly with every Templeton score, and watching the big numbers grimly as they steadily mounted on the opponent's side of the scoreboard. At the end of the first quarter, Templeton led, 19 to 13. Chip hadn't scored a point.

Corrigan gathered the players around him in front of the bench. "Listen, now," he whispered. "Chip is going back in and we're going to use the switch defense. That will enable Chip to switch off every time Johnson crosses with a teammate. Bill George will have his players keep the middle open to give Johnson room, but he will have to cross someone sooner or later and Chip can switch off. Try it, anyway."

Templeton's Coach George grinned and glanced at Corrigan when State's maneuver was apparent. It was evident that he had anticipated the move, because his players immediately reacted to the change in State's defense. When Johnson crossed and Chip switched to another opponent, *that* player immediately cut for the basket at full speed.

As soon as State got the ball again, Coach Corrigan called for another time-out. "We've got it now," he said confidently. "Rock figured it out. Johnson's the only *outside* shooter they have, the only player on their team who can hit from more than twenty feet. So, play him tight and float on the rest of them. That goes for Chip and everyone else. Got it?"

It worked! Chip played Johnson tight when he was forced to guard him, and his teammates did likewise. But when Chip switched off against one of the other Templeton players, he floated away and rested his knee. The switching helped offensively, too. It forced Templeton to change their defensive man-to-man alignment and Chip broke loose time after time for clear shots. He scored fourteen points in the six minutes he played, but Templeton led, 41 to 37, at the buzzer.

Chip played only six minutes in the third quarter and managed to hit for fifteen points, but Templeton was in the lead by seven at the end of the period, 61 to 54. Corrigan did not vary his tactics in the final quarter and it paid off. Chip got hot and his teammates fed him the ball every time they got their hands on the precious sphere. Chip hit consistently.

With twenty seconds left to play and Templeton leading 75 to 74, State held the ball for one shot, passing it around in the backcourt, maneuvering so Chip could make the try. With eight seconds left to play and every person in the field house on his feet, Markley dribbled to the free-throw line, pivoted, and gave Chip a beautiful hand-off as he drove for the basket. Johnson was caught by the pick, but his teammate switched and tried desperately to stop Chip's shot. He was a split second too slow and followed Chip toward the basket. Just as Chip went up for the lay-up, the frantic player crashed into Chip and knocked him to the floor. The referee's whistle barely beat the buzzer but there was no doubt about the foul. The official held up two fingers and motioned Chip to the free-throw line.

The pain in Chip's knee was excruciating now, but he gritted his teeth and made it to the line. A streak of fire was running up the side of his leg between the ankle and the thigh, and he bounced the ball several times while he tried to still the trembling muscles of his right leg.

Not a person in the great crowd made a sound; every fan was holding his breath. Chip bounced the ball once again and flipped the ball through the ring to tie the score at 75 to 75 with one more shot to come.

Chip managed a pain-riddled step back away from the line while the official was recovering the ball and looked toward the State bench. It was a flash glance, a desperate search for support from Soapy.

Chip couldn't see Soapy and the redhead was making no effort to see Chip. Soapy was leaning forward, screened by the standing players, resting his head on his arms which were draped over the chair in front of him; every fiber of his body tensed and straining as he held his breath and prayed for the booming crowd shout of exultation which would signify a successful shot.

In Valley Falls and back in University, thousands of Statesmen fans turned their eyes away from the television screen and waited and hoped for Gee-Gee Gray's cry of victory. . . .

The officials were signaling the crowd for silence as Chip stepped forward to the line and nearly collapsed. All strength seemed to have left his right knee and he stood there swaying slightly from side to side as he tried to support his weight on the other leg. The crowd gradually silenced, and when it was so still that Chip fancied that he could hear the throbbing in his knee, the official handed him the ball.

Chip had to put his weight on his bad leg to hold his balance, and nearly cried aloud with the pain. But he controlled the impulse and looked once more for Soapy. Soapy was in plain sight now, standing right on the edge of the floor, both fists doubled and chest held high. Despite the redhead's emotional stress, he had forced himself out in front to help his pal. His lips were moving soundlessly but Chip knew what Soapy was saying. And Chip felt he could make it good, too! . . .

And he did!

Yes, the ball went out and up and through the hoop so clean that it never touched the rim, barely rippled the cords. State had beaten Templeton 76 to 75, to gain the finals of the Holiday Invitational. Soapy was out on the floor almost as soon as the ball dropped through the net and Henry Rockwell and Murph Kelly were right beside him. They made a hand-chair and lifted Chip gently from the floor, just as he was surrounded by his teammates.

With Coach Corrigan and Doc Terring leading the way, they fought their way through the fans and through the aisle to the State dressing room. Bill Jenkins had the door already unlocked and barred the way to everyone except the coaches and players. The players immediately began to take the dressing room apart but sobered quickly enough when Murph Kelly bellowed for silence. "Chip's hurt, fellows! Quiet down!"

That brought a quick stillness to the room, all the more impressive because of the shouts and din from the hall and the frantic pounding on the door by the newspaper writers who wanted to see Chip Hilton. Twenty minutes later, when Doc Terring had completed his examination, they sat demoralized by the words of the kindly physician.

"Chip is through for the tournament!"

They sat stunned for a second. And then, as if it

just couldn't be true, they began to ply Doc Terring with questions. "You mean he can't play tomorrow against Southwestern?"

"Can't play in the *finals?*"

"You've got to be wrong, Doc! Just got to be!"

"I wish I was," Terring said sadly.

Chip was stunned, too. "Maybe it will be better tomorrow, Doc," he said hopefully.

Doc Terring shook his head. "Not a chance, Chip," he said kindly, placing a hand on Chip's shoulder. "You're a lucky youngster and you're going to stay that way."

Chip slid off the rubbing table to the floor. "Look, Doc," he said, sliding his right leg stiffly forward and assaying a step. "I can walk on it, all right."

Doc Terring grinned. "O.K.," he said, nodding, "so you can walk on it! But you're not going to do any running on it! And that's an order."

"Can I suit up for the game tomorrow night?"

"Well, maybe. Murph and I will see what we can work out in the way of a brace while you're taking your shower. Then we'll have a look."

The first quarter of the Southwestern-Tech game ended then and the writers were back. They overwhelmed Bill Jenkins and were firing questions at Doc Terring and Murph Kelly and Coach Corrigan when Chip finished his shower.

"You're sure he won't play tomorrow night?"

"Will he be in uniform?"

"How about an operation? Necessary?"

"If it's not *that* serious, why can't he play?"

"A ligament? Is that worse than a cartilage?"

"How can you strain a ligament?"

"I don't get it! He can walk but he can't run!"

"Oh, you mean they've stiffened up!"

"Wouldn't massage help? Couldn't the stiffness be rubbed or baked out? How about the whirlpool?"

"Seems a shame! Greatest shot I ever saw! Got forty-seven points tonight."

"And he only played twenty-four minutes!"

"Hey, you guys! Second quarter has started."

"Who cares? It's a walkaway! Southwestern is out in front by fifteen points."

It was a walkaway. Southwestern ended the half leading Tech by thirty points, 52 to 22, and kept pouring it on in the second half to win by a score of 94 to 61. Coach Jeff Habley never opened the gates of mercy for anyone. When the fans left the field house they were raving about the prowess of Southwestern and speculating on the showing the State star, Chip Hilton, would make against the champions.

Mr. Chang Lu Chung was beaming happily when he left the house Friday morning. The old gentleman moved slowly and graciously along, attracting some attention because of his stately bearing and dignified carriage. Yes, everything was right with Chang Lu Chung's world. His grandsons, Jimmy and Tommy, had risen with the sun and gone to work; his own son, Li Lu Chung, was once again in good health; the restaurant was a tremendous success, and certainly everything was working out just right for Jimmy's basketball friends. . . . Or so Chang Lu Chung thought. . . .

Chang Lu Chung purchased a morning paper at the corner and tucked it under his arm, keeping himself purposefully in suspense with respect to the outcome of the previous night's game. Not that he doubted the results. Hadn't he burned many candles

THROUGH FOR THE TOURNEY 193

to the Gods and Saints in behalf of Jimmy's basketball friends?

The old gentleman loved his grandsons deeply and lavished the affection upon them that he could not bestow on Li Lu Chung. And he knew their moods as well as his own. The two boys were waiting for him at the New Campus Inn and bowed a morning greeting. Chang's keen brown eyes immediately detected the gloom in their spirits.

"Beloved grandsons are distressed?"

Jimmy bowed again. "Honorable grandfather has not read the morning paper?"

"No, illustrious grandson. Will do so now." He proceeded to the office and opened the paper to the sports page. There, he read the full account of the game and all about Chip's injury and the terrific blow it was to State's chances against Southwestern. A few minutes later he left the restaurant without a word to his grandsons. They watched him through a street window. On the corner Chang Lu Chung hailed a taxi headed toward the center of the city.

The lobby of the Clinton Hotel was filled with basketball fans, players and coaches, and Chang Lu Chung was known by sight to some of them. These spoke, while others commented upon his tall, trim figure.

Soapy and Speed and Kirk Markley and Greg Moran were with Chip when Chang Lu Chung was admitted to the hotel room. He crossed the room quickly to the chair in which Chip was sitting and proffered his hand. "Young friend has experienced ill fortune. Chang Lu Chung is extremely concerned and hopes for a quick recovery. You are hurt badly?"

Chip smiled. "The injury itself isn't too serious, Mr. Lu Chung. I can move around as long as I don't run."

"You cannot play in the important game tonight?"

"No, Mr. Lu Chung. I guess I'll be out of basketball for some time."

Chang Lu Chung nodded slowly and studied the support strapped around Chip's knee. "You will be at game?"

"Yes, Mr. Lu Chung, I'll be there all right. I'll be in uniform, too, even though I can't play."

"I'll say he'll be there," Soapy said grimly. "We'll all be there—even if we have to crawl!"

"This is an important matter for all of you," Chang Lu Chung said, eying each of the boys. "This basketball championship."

"Yes, it is, Mr. Lu Chung," Chip said softly. "I wanted to play in this game more than any other in my life. It's important to the school and the coaches, but it's especially important to my friends."

Chang Lu Chung nodded. "I understand. Friendship means much to you. That is a fine thing. Friendship and the team spirit young friend Soapy was telling me about. They are extremely important.

"Well, young friend, I wish you a speedy recovery. And I agree with you that friendship is a priceless thing and is its own reward." He bowed and walked to the door, pausing with his hand on the knob. "Young friend Soapy also advised me of an axiom which I find most familiar. It goes something like: 'One for all and all for one.'"

He paused once more and then continued meaningly: "In Old China, a debt of one member of the family is a debt of all members of the family. . . . Good afternoon, illustrious friends."

CHAPTER 21

BEST IN BASKETBALL HISTORY

KIRK MARKLEY was bewildered. He waited until the door closed and then turned to Chip. "What's that all about? What does he mean 'Friendship is its own reward'?"

"He means we ought to be happy because the New Campus Inn is a big success!" Speed said bitterly. "Sure! Everything is just dandy! Chip and Soapy and Pete Thorp and Greg Moran and the rest of us work our heads off so we can get Jimmy back on the team and he gives us a lot of double talk! Friendship! Huh!"

"Take it easy, Speed," Chip remonstrated. "I think it was swell of him to come."

"Right!" Soapy added. "He's a wonderful man."

"Well, if he's so wonderful," Speed retorted, "why doesn't he tell Jimmy's father off? You said yourself, Chip, that he was the real boss of the family, the patriarchal father or whatever you call it. He sure doesn't act like it."

"He's got to be the boss," Chip said. "It just doesn't add up any other way."

Meanwhile, Chang Lu Chung had stopped in the

lobby of the hotel to pick up an afternoon paper which he read in the taxi on the way back to the New Campus Inn. He was especially thoughtful as he studied Chip's picture and read the article which was centered smack in the middle of the sports page.

FAMOUS STATE STAR SIDE-LINED

Southwestern Conceded Easy Championship Victory Tonight

Chip Hilton, leading Holiday Invitational Tournament scorer, suffered an injury to his knee last night which will force him to watch tonight's championship game between Southwestern and State from the side lines. Hilton scored 47 points last night and won the thrilling battle after the game was over. With ten seconds left to play and Templeton leading, 75 to 74, State's Kirk Markley passed to Hilton for a last-hope try for a score. Hilton took the pass and drove for the basket. Just as he released the ball, he was fouled.

Only a few of the 24,885 fans in Tech's giant field house realized that the famous star had been injured on the play. Hilton sank the two charity shots to make the score, State 76—Templeton 75, and put his team in the final championship game.

Later, in the State dressing room, it was discovered that Hilton was suffering from several pulled tendons and would not be able to compete tonight in the title game. The loss of the brilliant star makes State a hopeless underdog and most observers feel that Southwestern, the team the experts call the greatest in basketball history, will win in a walkaway and wrap up its fifth consecutive Holiday Invitational Tournament title. This observer feels that the victory margin can be measured only by the number of points Coach Jeff Habley feels necessary to humiliate his opponents. . . .

Chang Lu Chung thrust the paper aside and

tapped the taxi driver on the shoulder. "Please to change destination," he said.

Later that afternoon, when Chip limped into the New Campus Inn with Soapy and his teammates for the last meal before the championship game, every table, except that reserved for State, was filled. Li Lu Chung was standing just inside the entrance, but when he saw Soapy he walked clear to the other side of the dining room and watched his redheaded nemesis warily.

Jimmy and Tommy and Pete Thorp immediately dropped all other business and joined them. "How ya feeling, Champ?" Pete asked. "How's the leg?"

"Fine, Pete."

"You sure you can't play?"

"Absolutely. Doc Terring's orders. If we only had Jimmy . . ."

Pete glowered across the dining room at Li Lu Chung. "For two cents—" he began.

"I know," Chip said hastily. "Forget it!"

It was an awkward meal. Pete sat in a chair beside Chip, and Jimmy and Tommy seemed to have forgotten all about the other customers. Corrigan made the break, handing Jimmy a fistful of tickets. "Here's some tickets. They're right behind our bench. Try to make it. You too, Pete and Tommy. Well, wish us luck."

It was impossible to get near the Tech field house that night. Every street and sidewalk was jammed with fans. State's taxis were stopped at the main campus drive. Much to Corrigan's disgust, the policemen would not let them through. So they were forced to go the rest of the way on foot. Chip hobbled along behind with his teammates.

The main lobby was filled with a solid block of

unyielding humanity who resented every push until the State players were recognized. They reached the State dressing room finally and began to suit up. Chip tried to get out of dressing, but Coach Corrigan and his teammates wouldn't stand for it. "We're all in this together," Murph Kelly muttered, checking Chip's knee brace.

"That's right," Corrigan agreed. "And that means you, too, Smith. Got another uniform, Murph?"

"Jimmy's is the only one left, Coach."

"Give it to Soapy! He's earned it!"

Soapy's mouth fell open and he stared at Corrigan as if he couldn't believe his ears. "Me, Coach? Me?"

"Yes, you! Give him Lu Chung's suit, Murph. We want him on the bench for good luck. Seriously, Soapy, next to Chip, we all realize that no one has worked harder or done more to win this tournament than you. Right, gang?"

The cheer which the players gave Soapy then was a far greater reward than the happy-go-lucky redhead ever desired or expected. He gulped and shot a self-conscious glance at Chip. Chip was grinning and cheering with the rest and Soapy suddenly found it necessary to bend over and unlace one of his shoes. Then, while Soapy was suiting up, Coach Corrigan and Rock followed through with their old practice of moving from one player to the next with bits of advice and encouragement.

Someone banged on the door, then, and Bill Jenkins opened it an inch and peered out. Then he relayed the message: "We're due on the court for the pregame ceremonies in five minutes, Coach."

A violent banging on the door interrupted him and Corrigan turned impatiently to Jenkins. "Don't open the door!" he said sharply.

BEST IN HISTORY 199

Outside, there was a babble of voices and the pressure on the door increased, forcing Jenkins back. Corrigan was thoroughly upset now and gestured to Kelly. "Help him out, Murph. *No one* comes into this dressing room!"

"Hold it, Coach!" Soapy cried. "That's Mr. Lu Chung's voice! It's Jimmy, too!" He rushed to the door and pulled it open. Then he took one look and fell back in amazement. "Mr. Lu Chung!" he gasped.

This was a night of surprises, but no one was prepared for the sight which met his eyes when Mr. Chang Lu Chung stepped into the room. His tall, erect figure was clad in a stylish, midnight-gray suit, and he wore a white shirt, a black striped tie, a black Homburg hat, and he carried a cane. He smiled at Coach Corrigan and doffed the hat, and for the first time the startled players noticed that his mustache and beard were gone. Crowding in behind him came Mr. Li Lu Chung, Tommy Lu Chung, Pete Thorp, and Jimmy.

"Jimmy!" Chip cried, forgetting his leg and leaping forward. "You're going to play!"

"Friend Chip Hilton speaks correctly," Chang Lu Chung said calmly. "The Lu Chung family much appreciates what young friend Soapy said about 'One for all and all for one' and it is hoped young grandson's humble efforts may partly repay his debt to such illustrious friends. A debt of one member of the Lu Chung family is a debt of all."

Corrigan was the first to recover from the shock. He grabbed Kelly by the arm. "Give him a suit, Murph. Quick!"

"But I haven't got a suit—"

"Whaddaya mean you haven't got a suit?" Soapy demanded, pulling Jimmy's shirt over his head and tossing it in Jimmy's direction. "Whaddaya call this?"

Confusion reigned. Mr. Chang Lu Chung and Mr. Li Lu Chung were trying to help Jimmy undress, speaking in Chinese, and doing more to handicap than help him, while the rest of the players stared with unbelieving eyes at the mad action.

Then the game buzzer cut through the turmoil and Corrigan led the players toward the court, shouting over his shoulder: "Hurry up Murph. We're starting Jimmy in place of Tucker."

Somehow, someway, Murph Kelly got Jimmy suited up. Soapy was so excited he couldn't find his shirt and Kelly made him slip on a warm-up jacket with a big 50 on the back.

"It's an omen!" Soapy cried. "Southwestern's after game number fifty and I've got it on my back! That's one number they'll never get!"

"Come on!" Kelly growled. "We got a job to do!" He led the way and made a place on the State bench for Mr. Chang Lu Chung, Mr. Li Lu Chung, Tommy Lu Chung, Pete Thorp, Soapy, and Chip. Out on the court, the pregame ceremonies had been completed and Jimmy had joined in the State warm-up drill. His presence created a stir among the fans and writers, and Coach Corrigan sent Henry Rockwell over to the score table to make sure Jimmy was entered in the scorebook and to explain his presence to the writers.

Fortunately, Jimmy's name had never been removed from the roster and the fans quickly identified him. Jimmy made his presence known quickly enough but the program helped. When the two teams lined up for the opening center tap, Southwestern towered over the State players like a college squad over an eighth-grade public-school team.

BEST IN HISTORY 201

Surprisingly, Sky Bollinger got the tap. Bordon took it easy and State was away, all five players breaking for the basket like runaway horses. Sky took a pass from Bitsy Reardon and scored before Bordon got out of the center circle. But that was just the start. During the next three minutes, Kirk Markley was the only State player to drop back under the Southwestern basket on defense.

Jimmy Lu Chung, Speed Morris, Bitsy Reardon, and Sky Bollinger met the bewildered champions in the State end of the court three straight times and stole the ball three times for three easy baskets. The four speedsters dashed wildly after the ball, double-teaming opponents when possible, switching when necessary, and playing for an interception on every pass.

The fans rose to their feet en masse when Jimmy stole a pass right out of Rip Ralk's hands and dribbled all alone under the State basket for another unguarded shot. That made the score: State 10, Southwestern 0, and Jeff Habley bellowed for a time-out.

The crowd noise never slackened during the time-out. State's race-horse tactics were as much a surprise to the fans as they were to the national champions. Jeff Habley was raging in the huddle of players in front of the Southwestern bench, shaking a fist under the noses of his players and yelling at the top of his voice.

It helped the champions a little, but it was obvious to every fan in the field house that Southwestern had been caught asleep. Then they made a bad mistake, the mistake Chip had figured they might make. They tried to outrun State. The effort rebounded and the game became a runaway scoring match, with all science and all thoughts of defense flying out the window. Despite Jeff Habley's berating shouts and mad bellowing, he could not control his players.

Jimmy was sensational. He was all over the court, making unbelievable interceptions, setting up scoring plays for his teammates, and, in the process, scoring thirty-seven points himself. State led 62 to 53 at the half, and the crowd was still cheering Jimmy and his teammates minutes after they went to the dressing room.

Jimmy put his arm around Chip and they walked back to the dressing room together with Soapy leading the way, elbowing a path through the fans who were trying to get a good look at Jimmy and Chip.

Inside the dressing room, Coach Corrigan and Henry Rockwell and Murph Kelly were working furiously over the players, almost as excited as the fans who thronged the hall outside the door. Corrigan didn't say very much when it was time to go back out on the floor. There wasn't much he could say. But he did warn them that Southwestern was a great ball club and reminded them of the great spurt the champions had taken in the second half of the "treatment game."

"Only twenty minutes to go, gang! Don't back up an inch! How are you feeling, Jimmy? Good! All right, same team! No changes and no letdown! Now go get 'em!"

They filed out through the crowd in the aisle, and as they passed the Southwestern dressing room they could hear Coach Jeff Habley yelling at the top of his voice. The fans blocked their way, calling encouragement and trying to get as close to the Cinderella Team as possible.

"That's Hilton! Too bad he couldn't play tonight!"

"Must have been keeping this Lu Chung under wraps!"

"This is gonna be the biggest upset in the history of basketball!"

"It's not over yet. Southwestern's a second-half ball club."

"Sure didn't look like champions the first half!"

"Be different now. Habley will fire 'em up! But good!"

Coach Corrigan glanced at the time clock and sent the State players out on the court to line up. They stood there until the referee waved them back to their bench and sent the umpire for Southwestern. But the umpire came right back, shaking his head and said something to the referee. Then Coach Corrigan sent State back out on the court and this time the referee went to the Southwestern dressing room himself. And when the champions finally did appear, the referee penalized them with a technical foul.

Then Coach Habley really put on an act, kicking over the bucket of water in front of his bench and yelling at the officials at the top of his voice. And he was still yelling when Kirk Markley dropped the ball through the hoop to give State a ten-point lead, 63 to 53.

Coach Habley's side-line actions seemed to set the pattern for the Southwestern players, for they began to use their rough stuff. Munn sent Jimmy sprawling with a shove just as the referee tossed up the ball. The act went undetected and Chip watched Jimmy anxiously, fearing he might fall into the trap and lose his head. But Jimmy glanced over at Chip and winked. Chip breathed a sigh of relief. Jimmy knew the score. . . .

It was a rough, tough, knock-'em-down, drag-out period, and Southwestern slowly but surely closed the gap. The officials didn't let the game get out of hand; kept calling the fouls and these kept State in the game. At the end of the third quarter, State led: 87 to 85.

Coach Jeff Habley was on his feet with every call in the fourth quarter, protesting and yelling and shaking his fist at the officials, and these tactics drew two technical fouls. But the champions were aroused now, played desperately, and their weight and height and endurance began to tell. They caught up, tied the score, and then went out in front by five points, 103 to 98, with four minutes left to play.

Then, just when the State cause seemed hopeless, Jimmy stole the ball twice in a row while Southwestern was attempting a freeze and scored both times. That brought the Statesmen back into contention, only a point behind, with the score Southwestern 103—State 102, and Jeff Habley called for a time-out.

Jimmy was out on his feet and Coach Corrigan used his last time-out as soon as the Southwestern time-out ended. "That's it, gang," he said. "We've used our last one, so for goodness sakes don't ask for another one."

There was two minutes and two seconds left to play when Ralk and Munn brought the ball upcourt. All the drive had gone out of Sky Bollinger and Kirk Markley and Speed Morris and the press was impossible. Only Jimmy and Bitsy still possessed the reserve strength to keep pressing and it was Jimmy who dove for the ball and forced Munn to make a bad pass. The ball was just out of Ralk's reach but his fingers got enough of the ball to deflect it out of

BEST IN HISTORY 205

bounds in front of the Southwestern bench. Then Jeff Habley made a disastrous mistake. Almost as if by instinct, without seemingly giving it a thought, the excited man sprang to his feet and pushed Jimmy roughly away from the ball. And as Jimmy recovered and leaped for the ball, Habley kicked it.

Every fan in the field house gasped at the audacity and stupidity of the man. The referee was so surprised and shocked that he was late in blowing his whistle. But he called the technical foul and pointed to Habley, and walked briskly to the State free-throw line.

Habley shouted for another time-out, and when his players gathered in front of the bench, he ignored them completely and began yelling at the officials. Coach Corrigan took advantage of the time-out to talk to his team. "Shoot it, Markley," he said.

"I can't, Coach. I'm all in! I'll miss it!"

Corrigan glanced around the circle of tired, drawn faces and made a sudden decision. "Chip!" he called. "Quick! Report for Markley! Shoot the free throw!"

Before Chip could catch his breath, Henry Rockwell lifted him to his feet. "You've got to do it, Chip. The team needs you now. Make the shot, Chip, and then take the ball out of bounds. Pass it in and stay out of the play. Got it? And, Chip— A little higher and a little harder."

A tremendous cheer greeted Chip as he stripped off his warm-up jacket and limped to the scoring table. And it grew in volume as he made it to the free-throw line and took the ball. He glanced at the scoreboard: Southwestern 103, State 102.

Chip felt it was all a dream. He moved his feet into position, making sure that the toes of his shoes did not infringe upon the free-throw line, and glanced at the basket. Then he bounced the ball and concentrated on the spot on the rim. The tension of the crowd seemed to move in and envelop him like the fog of a dark, misty night.

And as Chip bounced the ball, it seemed he could hear Henry Rockwell saying, "When you're tired and tight and jittery, Chip, shoot a little higher and a little harder and make sure you follow through with your hands."

The crowd felt the suspense, now, and the shouts and cheers became a steady roar. The official stepped in front of Chip and held up his hands for silence. It was to no avail. No one could have silenced the roar of that crowd. He waited several seconds and then shrugged his shoulders and stepped back out of the lane. "Take your time, son," he said. "I can't do anything with them."

Chip bounced the ball twice, took a deep breath, and aimed the ball. Then he let it go, a little higher and a little harder and with a little more follow-through. The ball went spinning up and out and down through the hoop and swished through the cords to tie the score!

The big numbers on the scoreboard blinked hard and fast and off and on and there it was: Southwestern 103, State 103.

Pandemonium! Thundering bombilation and turmoil! A deafening and tumultuous roar of relief, frustration, anguish, and joy. Then it dwindled as the drama on the floor brought realization that the issue was still in doubt.

CHAPTER 22

PICTURES, CUPS, AND WATCHES

GEE-GEE GRAY was going to town up in the broadcasting booth. "It's State's ball out of bounds, now. Hilton is going to pass it in. The ball is dead until it touches a player on the court, you know—

"Hilton fakes to Morris and throws the ball to Bollinger—the big center leaps high in the air— Oh, no!

"Bollinger fumbled Hilton's pass, fans. Bordon has the ball now. He passes it over to Ralk and the great All-American passes it over to Lloyd and drives toward the basket. Hilton is limping down the court —he can't keep up with Ralk.

"Stuff Lloyd and Joe Munn are bringing the ball upcourt—Munn glances at the clock to make sure there is plenty of time. Every fan in this big field house—twenty-five thousand of them—shifts his eyes to follow Munn's glance.

"Televiewers, ladies and gentlemen, the attunement of the fans here tonight to the action out on the court has been complete ever since State unveiled its bewildering press attack.

"Through all the fury of this great game, every person in this building has avidly followed the brilliant play of these two great teams. Most of the spectators here can hardly believe what they are seeing.

"Over to Lloyd—back to Munn—in to Bordon! Two-Ton fakes a shot and passes out to Ralk. The famous star pivots away from Hilton and holds the ball while he checks the time.

"Ninety seconds to go!

"Both benches have emptied now—the players and coaches are standing on the edge of the court, pressing forward in their agonizing desire to help their teammates.

"The Southwestern players are chanting: 'Hold that ball! Hold that ball!' And right beside them, almost shoulder to shoulder, completely blocking off the scoring table, the State players are screaming: 'Get the ball! Get the ball!'

"Coach Jeff Habley is running from one end of the bench to the other. He's lost all control of himself. He's calling every play! I can hear him bellow clear up here! He's pointing from one player to the other, signaling every pass."

Through the roar, Chip could hear the famous coach shouting: "Ralk! Watch out! You hear me, Ralk? Give the ball to Perkins! Over to Munn, now, Joe. You hear, Joe? Pass and cut away. *Away* from the ball!"

Chip glanced at the clock. Sixty seconds left . . . If he could only call a time-out. He gave Ralk a little more room, backed up, waited with bated breath. And the same words were running through his thoughts time after time: "If Ralk cuts now, I'm lost. . . ."

PICTURES, CUPS, WATCHES 209

Gee-Gee Gray was leaning over the side of the broadcasting box, every fiber of his being tingling with the excitement of the tense climax. "Joe Munn flips the ball to Perkins—Perkins fakes a return pass and chucks the ball to Ralk. Ralk catches the ball and pivots away from Hilton. He holds the ball at arm's length while he studies the clock. It is a magnificent display of confidence."

Down on the side line, in front of the Southwestern bench, Coach Jeff Habley was still bellowing: "One shot, Rip! Hold it! One shot! Hold that ball! Hear me, Rip? Watch out! Give it to Lloyd!"

From the State bench, heart-rending pleas and shouts: "Go get *that* ball!" "*Do* something! Don't just stand there! You've *got* to *do* something!"

Gray was spelling the story out over his mike to millions of listeners and his quick eyes caught every move on the court.

"Ralk glances tantalizingly over his shoulder at Hilton and jerks the ball back as if threatening to throw it in the injured State star's face—it's just a gesture—of course. He's ignoring Hilton now. Now Ralk zips the ball toward Stuff Lloyd."

On the court, taut and keyed to an almost heartbreaking pitch, Jimmy had been playing dummy against Stuff Lloyd. What happened then was so unexpected that most of the fans missed the play entirely.

Jimmy shot forward like a flash of light. The lunge of his body and the desperate thrust of his hand was too fast to be seen. But he hit the ball!

Stuff Lloyd had expected the pass and had dropped back toward the ten-second line. But, too late, he had seen Jimmy poise for the interception. "No!" he shouted. "No, Rip! Watch out!" Then he turned and dashed for the State basket still shouting, "No! No!"

Twenty-five thousand voices rose in a thundering crescendo to testify to the interception.

Gee-Gee Gray had seen the play, had found himself shouting, his voice vibrant with emotion. "Lu Chung slips; he goes to one knee—now he's up and driving forward! He slaps the ball again—the precious sphere bounces. Lu Chung is over it now and the ball is responding to the deftness of his touch as if it is on a string.

"Ralk is standing as if paralyzed, fans. He's trying to fight back the realization that Lu Chung has stolen the ball and is on his way toward the State basket. He takes off after Lu Chung, ignoring Hilton completely.

"Lloyd is ahead of Lu Chung—he's got a ten-foot start over his opponent as he heads diagonally for the basket—Lloyd is fast and his long legs are edging him ahead of Lu Chung.

"Lu Chung swerves away and I can hear the sigh of the Southwestern rooters clear up here in the broadcasting booth. It's like the steam release of a huge locomotive.

"Lu Chung is dribbling away from Lloyd now—toward the side of the court. The crowd is quieting a bit.

"Southwestern is back on defense now and Rip Ralk has paired up against Lu Chung. Munn made a move away from Chip Hilton just now, fans, but he moved back when Hilton hobbled toward the open basket. Ralk is on his own again—he can't catch his elusive opponent.

"It's no contest, fans! Ralk is discouraged . . ."

PICTURES, CUPS, WATCHES

Chip was trying to keep Munn out of Jimmy's way and caught only a glimpse of Jimmy's maneuvers. But he heard the giant wave of applause from friend and foe alike and heard it pick up in volume and sweep down and around the court as Jimmy toyed with Ralk and played for time.

Chip checked the time, keeping his eyes focused on the clock. Fifteen seconds . . . fourteen seconds . . .

Jimmy's eyes were fixed on the clock, too. And he kept up his dribbling: tap-tap, tappity-tap, tap-tap, guiding the precious ball with his supple fingers. The ball bounced this way and that, forward and back, and left and right, as if it was the shadow of his hand. And through it all, Jimmy was seemingly oblivious to Ralk, expressed no obvious desire to humiliate his furious opponent.

Chip was counting aloud now: "Nine seconds! Eight! Seven! . . ."

Then Jimmy maneuvered to the right, faked back, and then drove to the right . . .

And while Chip was counting and hoping and pulling for his friend with all his heart, Jimmy dribbled behind his back and cut in the opposite direction. Ralk made a final desperate lunge for the ball but it was a futile gesture.

Jimmy took off from the free-throw line and let the shot go just as the big second hand made its final move. Chip tried to follow the flight of the ball but he never saw it drop through the hoop; heard only the tremendous crowd roar. Then his teammates dashed out on the court just as the buzzer sounded ending the game!

Yes, the ball flew straight and sure and never

touched the rim; swished through the cords as if it had eyes, just as the buzzer drilled through the deafening roar.

State had accomplished the impossible; had tumbled mighty Southwestern to its first defeat after forty-nine consecutive victories, and had won the Holiday Invitational Tournament: State 105, Southwestern 103.

Hysteria gripped almost everyone in the arena, notable exceptions being Chang Lu Chung and Li Lu Chung. They sat immobile, inscrutable and calm, watching the mad antics of the fans and players as if unable to understand the why or wherefore of the scene. Out on the court, the jubilant State players had lifted Jimmy to their shoulders and were already surrounded by fans. And then they swarmed back and hoisted Soapy with the big 50 on the back of his warm-up jacket to their shoulders. Then they joined the mob on the floor.

Many of the fans were amazed at this development. "Wonder what that's all about?" they cried.

"Why *he* wasn't in the game!"

"Number fifty isn't even listed in the program!"

Inside the dressing room, the triumphant warriors unceremoniously dumped Jimmy and Soapy under the shower and gave Chip and Chang Lu Chung and Li Lu Chung a resounding cheer.

Corrigan and Rockwell made the mistake of rushing in to join the celebration at that moment and they, too, ended up under the shower—clothes and all!

There was a great pounding at the door and the tournament officials and several policemen barged into the dressing room. "You fellows are wanted out on the floor!" the excited director shouted.

PICTURES, CUPS, WATCHES 213

"They're waiting to give you the prizes. You won the tournament! Or didn't you know?"

"Yes," another added. "And that means pictures and cups and watches! C'mon! Can't you hear the crowd? They're waiting for you, Champs!"

Seconds later, when the soaking wet Holiday Invitational Tournament champions walked out on Tech's preciously polished floor, a great cheer greeted them. And it exploded and boomed out into the hall where Chip Hilton, flanked on both sides by Chang Lu Chung and Li Lu Chung, was being unnecessarily escorted toward the court.

The fans were subjected to another surprise on this great night of upsets when Chang Lu Chung and Li Lu Chung walked Chip right out before the table where all the prizes rested. The director's voice drilled through the loud-speaker then, announcing that the tournament committee had found it difficult to select one player as the most valuable.

"We have, therefore," the director said, "been forced to select two great players from the same team and they will be awarded identical cups! Ladies and gentlemen, athletes, coaches, fans, I give you Chip Hilton and Jimmy Lu Chung!"

The New Campus Inn was jammed. Every seat was taken and every inch of space along the walls was lined with fans and customers and college boys and girls all joining in the hilarious celebration and waiting eagerly for Soapy Smith's New Year's Eve party to begin.

In the middle of the main dining room, the State basketball team and other celebrities were ensconced at a long table covered with favors and horns and sandwiches and cakes and relishes and salads and cold cuts and fruit and nuts and so many other delicacies that even Pete Thorp and Tommy Lu Chung couldn't name them.

And right in the center of the table, the big championship bowl was sitting up on a box for all the world to see, with ribbons leading to all the places on the table.

Chip and Jimmy were seated on each side of Gee-Gee Gray in the seats of honor. Li Lu Chung and Chang Lu Chung were next, and then around the table were Coach Jim Corrigan, Henry Rockwell, Doc Terring, Murph Kelly, Toots Chandler, Greg Moran, Kirk Markley, Randy Thornhill, Biz Gowdy, Butcher King, Dom Di Santis, Sky Bollinger, Rud Slater, Speed Morris, Reb Tucker, Bitsy Reardon, and Bill Jenkins, the manager. Pete Thorp and Tommy Lu Chung hovered over the table, worried that some of their guests might feel slighted.

The din was deafening, but somehow Gee-Gee Gray got the guests to quiet down and the speechmaking began. Gee-Gee called on Chip and Jimmy and Corrigan and Soapy and Markley and Thornhill and Murph Kelly and Toots Chandler. Toots got a big hand when he said: "Don't forget, Tech won third place!"

Then Gray introduced Li Lu Chung. The proprietor of the New Campus Inn had difficulty finding the right words and some of the fans couldn't hear him, but every syllable came through to Chip Hilton as clear as a bell.

"You happy to know," Mr. Lu Chung said, smiling happily, "young Number Two son, Tommy, is taking over as manager of New Campus Inn while eldest son, Jimmy, pursue education and basketball at State."